DOLPHIN'S CAVE

DOLPHIN'S CAVE

By D. L. Finn

Library of Congress Control Number: *2017910204*

Cover: Monica Gibson

ISBN PRINT: **978-0-9977519-2-5**
ISBN EBOOK: 978-0-9977519-3-2

D. L. Finn
www.dlfinnauthor.com
D. C. Hawk Publishing

Chapter 1
In Her Dreams

Darkness came as it did every evening—quietly and completely. Slumber always brought the same dreams ever since Coral Dover's parents' plane had disappeared off the radar en route from Oahu to Maui. Coral never gave up hope that her parents were somewhere waiting to be found. Her faith had been solid for eight long years, but now it was eroding like rocky sea cliffs, constantly being battered by the ocean's salty reality. Her escape was her dreams. Every night the same events replayed, but they seemed new every time—like dream-state amnesia. Covers over her head and eyes tightly shut, sleep engulfed her as she sank into hope.

***

The ocean water was warm as she swam away from the protected cove of a black sandy beach. Suddenly a painless grasp at her legs pulled her underwater. There was no fear, only curiosity. The deeper she went, the cooler the water became, yet she wasn't cold. More important, though, she wasn't fighting to breathe.

Eyes burning from the saltwater, she couldn't see who or what pulled her. Abruptly she was released and settled into a neutral buoyancy. Surroundings came into focus. The blue encased her, and there was no way to tell which way was up. Goosebumps covered her arms, and she turned around. She saw a turtle and a dolphin—her kidnappers.

The turtle held back while the dolphin moved in and nudged her leg with its snout and then turned away from her. It was ten feet long, dark gray on top fading to white underneath. She knew it was a bottlenose dolphin thanks to her mom, who had written and illustrated a children's book called *What's Swimming in the Hawaiian Sea?*

Coral used to insist that her mom read her newly published book to her before bed. This turtle looked exactly like the one in the book—a green sea

- 1 -

turtle, or honu, as the Hawaiians called it. It was brown and about three feet wide. Unsure what to do next, she watched the turtle and let the memories surface.

"The turtle's name comes from its adult diet of seagrass and other plants, which are stored in its fat and turn it green. The color isn't external, but internal." A warm smile danced across her mom's face. "Wouldn't it be nice if everyone was judged by the color of their fat, or what was on the inside and not the outside?"

Waves of her past washed over her every time she thought about her parents. Instead of drowning in her pain, she was kept afloat by the hope of one day seeing them.

The dolphin nudged her with its nose again, bringing her back to this dream reality. Its expression looked like a smile. She knew there was a mouthful of teeth behind that smile that the dolphin used to catch food. Coral was caught. The dolphin nodded its head, then swam under her and waited. Carefully and gently she touched its fin. The dolphin showed no signs of being upset by her touch. It didn't attempt to bite or release a burst of bubbles from its blowhole. Both good signs, yet she held back.

The dolphin took control and pushed up under her. And just like that, she was riding it. She clung to its dorsal fin as it swam, surfacing every seven minutes to breathe. She almost slipped off a few times, but the dolphin slowed and maneuvered so that she could adjust herself. Unlike the dolphin, who breathed air, Coral was able to breathe both air and water.

How am I doing this?

Bewildered, she focused on what was occurring, how the water entered new slits on her neck and exited through her nose. When they broke the water's surface, she took in air through her nose or mouth. The dolphin's process was different. It blew out its used air from a blowhole on top of its head when it surfaced, sounding much like a balloon quickly losing air. Then it sucked air in through the same hole and refilled its lungs. Coral's intake of air was quiet yet dramatic as she switched from water to air.

The dolphin stopped and waited in the sunlight, which was blinding. Coral's eyes watered from the salt while they slowly adjusted. There was a small island off to the right, and the dolphin swam in that direction. There were no hotels or people around. Was she going to be stranded here, or was there another purpose? A knowing poured through her. Her parents were stranded somewhere and couldn't get back to her.

There was no sand on this shoreline, only jagged black rocks from years of volcanic eruptions. They were heading for the tallest cliff when the turtle bumped against her leg.

"Where are we going?"

They swam right up to the cliff.

"Are my parents here?"

The dolphin dove into the clear blue water. A school of bright yellow-and-blue fish swam by, and Coral saw an underwater cave straight ahead. Her grip tightened on the dolphin's fin as they swam into it. She could see lights ahead. Finally they were about to surface, and she'd have some answers—

***

Coral shot up in bed as she grasped her surroundings. Wide awake and thirsty, she reached for the always-present glass of water next to her bed and finished it in three large gulps. The cool liquid soothed her dry throat and washed away the salty taste in her mouth. Her thirst was quenched, and the dream kept the hope alive that her parents were waiting for her in that cave. Unfortunately, she always woke up before a reunion.

She frowned and glanced at the red numbers reflected on her ceiling: 2:00 a.m. She sighed. The next dream would have to wait. Memories started to flood her thoughts.

She could hear Aunt Ruby's voice as clearly as if she were right there in the room with her. "I'm sorry, Coral, but as much as I would like it to be true, your parents aren't coming home. Your dream isn't real. Their plane crashed, and we lost them. We have to let them go and move on."

The logical part of Coral knew that her aunt was right. She'd been sent to three different therapists, who all voiced the same sentiment. The first one wanted Aunt Ruby to take Coral to Hawaii to see where her parents had disappeared. Coral would be better able to process their loss, the therapist had explained. Aunt Ruby nixed that suggestion and found a second therapist who wanted to try hypnosis to convince Coral of the same thing after a few sessions. Aunt Ruby refused and made the final switch to Lilly, therapist number three. By then Coral had figured out what she had to do so they'd leave her small, illogical hope alone.

"It's a breakthrough!" Lilly had told Aunt Ruby when she picked Coral up after her session.

"I know she doesn't want to believe it. Neither do I, but I am glad she finally accepts it."

"Yes, we made great progress today. Your niece realizes her dream was a way of keeping her parents alive. She's ready to come once a month now to check in and talk about anything that's bothering her."

Lilly smiled so broadly she looked like a shark. Coral shuddered. Was there another side to her pleasant therapist?

"Great. Thank you, Doctor."

Although Coral didn't see that evil smile again, she was still glad she only had to see Lilly once a month. Had her dream returned? Everything else okay? The right answers always got her out of the office faster. Coral was over discussing her feelings with strangers. The people she did want to share her dreams with were Tara—her best friend—and Mr. Penny.

Mr. Penny had taken her aside once in private. "I have to speak up, at least to you. These therapists—and, I'm sorry to say, your aunt too—are wrong. Just like your mom, I believe dreams are valuable. See what comes next in your dream, Coral. It might be important, but at least it will give you closure, right? Dreams have never hurt anyone that I've ever known."

Mr. Penny had been her dad's best friend since their time in the air force together, and she trusted him. Although he wasn't a general anymore, some still called him that, but he would always be Mr. Penny to her. He worked with her parents and aunt at Dunning Corporation, an ocean research company. Coral had no idea what they did there, but she found it odd that they did it in the middle of a desert. She tried asking her aunt about it once.

Aunt Ruby had shaken her head. "I can't talk about my job, Coral. You know that—I don't know why you keep asking. My answer isn't going to change. Just be happy that I have a good-paying job and leave it at that."

"But I'm family, and my parents worked there too."

"Yes, but rules are rules." Aunt Ruby had crossed her arms, which meant the discussion was over.

"Well, if you can't talk about your job, can we at least go on a vacation to the ocean?"

"You know I can't get time off for a vacation like that. There's so much going on at work. But soon we can take a trip to Tahoe, or maybe just hang out in Reno. We always have fun doing that, right?"

"Yes." Coral had reluctantly agreed, but she wasn't going to give up. Ever.

In the meantime she was stuck in the middle of the Nevada desert, an hour out of Reno and at least six hours from any ocean, in a little town called Scuttle Valley. Her mom had loved that name, said it was the best-named town in the world. Her dad had laughed at that, but Coral never understood why it was so funny. Maybe it was a cute old cowboy town for visitors, but Coral thought it was awfully boring, and she'd made that known to her aunt more than once. She quickly learned that expressing this opinion only landed her with things to do, and not fun things, either.

Coral groaned. It was now 3:02, and she was still wide awake. Her aunt would expect her up early to get caught up on chores or whatever she had planned for Saturday morning. She flipped on her side to stare at the moon because her mind wasn't allowing her to go back to sleep. It was taking her in so many directions, like a tilt-a-whirl.

She pictured her mom's beautiful face and wished she looked more like her. The only feature she'd inherited from her was her startling green eyes. She had her dad's dark brown hair, but it was her aunt she really took after. They were both tall and thin and the only ones who needed glasses.

She yawned and turned away from her window, pulling the covers high over her head like a cocoon. Her heavy thoughts drifted back into the night, knowing what was coming next—her second dream.

***

Coral was so excited! For the first time, she was going to see where her parents worked. They pointed out the ten-story building. Her parents had to be important to work in such a place. Her mom and dad boarded a tan-and-orange plane with the Dunning Corporation logo on the side. It reminded her of a large orange beehive. She smiled widely as her parents turned and waved. Her mom blew a kiss. They'd be gone for four long days on their business trip, and Coral missed them already.

The plane built up speed as it thrust into the air. She clasped her new dolphin necklace in her hand. It had been a gift for her seventh birthday— the day before. There'd been a note inside the box telling her that this summer they would take a family vacation to Hawaii. Along with her Aunt Ruby, they would take a boat cruise to see dolphins living the way they were supposed to—free. The dolphin necklace was a reminder that in only a couple of months, she'd be in a tropical paradise.

Coral blew a final kiss to the departing plane. As soon as it disappeared into the horizon, Aunt Ruby grabbed her hand. They left without seeing any more of her parents' workplace.

She could barely sleep that night, thinking about finally getting to see the ocean. The dolphins would leap high out of the sea. She'd swim with them in the warm tropical water. Her family always went on good vacations, like camping in Tahoe or renting a houseboat on Lake Shasta or Lake Mead, but Hawaii was Coral's dream vacation. Tomorrow she'd ask Aunt Ruby to help her count the days until their trip, and she'd put an X on the calendar to cross off each one.

It was late that night when she managed to fall asleep on the stiff, white sheets in her aunt's guest bedroom. Her dreams carried her to pristine beaches meeting the blue ocean.

The next morning came abruptly. Aunt Ruby rushed into the spare bedroom with swollen eyes full of tears. She solemnly told Coral that her parents' plane had been lost at sea. Where they had gone down was classified information, but it was near Maui. They were gone.

Chapter 2
Good News!

T he second dream always ended there. Coral wiped away her tears. No matter how many times she had this dream, it always made her sad. Nothing had been the same since the day her parents went missing. A part of her always believed that they weren't dead, even though their house was sold, their belongings gone. Now she lived in a two-bedroom condo with her aunt. None of the material stuff mattered, though, and she clung to what others considered wishful thinking. She promised herself that one day she would go to Hawaii, to the place where her parents' plane had disappeared. Reaffirming that promise, she drifted back into a dreamless sleep.

***

Sabella sighed. Every evening she watched her beautiful granddaughter sleep in the air people's world. She sent the same dreams so Coral wouldn't give up or forget her mom. Time was running out because Coral's change was coming. Not only was Sabella aware of this, but those cruel air people also knew. She had learned a painful lesson when it came to the air people. She no longer took chances when it came to family, but this time she had to depend on her enemies to deliver what was most precious. There was no other choice.

She peered through a blue-tinted window and studied her beloved golden city. It was her deepest wish that she could deliver the same hope to her daughter, Ruby. The air world had consumed her. Ruby had not only forgotten who she was but lost the ability to receive dreams. Sabella's only interaction with her was through Ruby's own dreams.

Sabella sighed right as Tillie whizzed by her window. The little blue dragon was a favorite in the realm—like its young master—and could usually erase her dire moods, but not this time. She closed the heavy blue velvet drapes and sank into bed as her carefully contained grief burst through like a river overflowing its banks. Soon, she consoled herself, Coral and Ruby would be in her arms. Brushing away her tears, she closed her eyes to sleep while Coral was opening her eyes in the other world—the world of the air people.

***

"Coral! Breakfast!" Aunt Ruby removed any hope of sleeping in.

"Coming." Coral rubbed her eyes and stretched.

A glance at her clock showed it was not even seven. She moaned but rolled out of bed, threw on some clothes, grabbed her glasses, and ran her fingers through her hair before sinking into the brown leather chair at the table across from her aunt. Over their usual quiet breakfast of cereal and orange juice, Aunt Ruby made a shocking announcement.

"We're finally going to get a real vacation, Coral." She stirred cream into her coffee.

"Vacation?"

"Yes." Aunt Ruby avoided eye contact as she pushed the printout for two plane tickets across the round glass table. The paper stopped next to Coral's bowl brimming with colorful circles and marshmallows.

Coral's hand shook as she picked them up. "Hawaii?" She put her spoon down and studied her aunt.

"Yes. Although it's business for Mr. Penny and me, you'll be able to spend some time with Beth, Ben, and Mrs. Penny. We'll leave next week for Christmas break. Good thing we haven't decorated for the holidays yet. We can get our presents in Hawaii."

Aunt Ruby looked happy! Wow! She never looked happy.

"Right." Coral's mouth hung open.

"Yes, right! This is going to be a memorable Christmas for us. We'll go clothes shopping today, just as soon as you finish your breakfast and run a brush through your hair."

"Cool!"

"Yes, it is."

Who was this bubbly person sitting in front of her? The drab, rule-following aunt she'd come to know was gone. Coral choked down the rest of her soggy cereal, loaded her bowl and spoon into the dishwasher, and rushed to her room.

She scrutinized the girl in the mirror. Her aunt was right about her hair—it looked like an octopus reaching out in all directions. She remedied that with a quick ponytail. Her face was flushed, and her eyes stared back in disbelief. It was happening! She stuffed her cell phone into her purse and brushed her teeth. The tug of a restless night was gone.

Hurrying to her aunt's truck, deep in thought, she texted Tara the great news. *We are going to Hawaii for Christmas. Can you believe it? The only downside is going with the Penny family.*

Tara responded immediately. *Awesome. You'll have so much fun. I know you've said they both seem like they belong on the Oregon Trail, but I envy you.*

I know. But I wish you were going with us instead.

I wish I could go with you too, but New York calls. I plan on both of us making it to New York next year. You know they blew it not including you this time. You're just as good a dancer as I am. Whatever, it's their loss. Anyways, after graduation, we can plan a trip to Hawaii. Start saving. And you know I like Ben, so whatever you could do to move him along with that.

Coral sighed. *Sure, next time. I'll definitely start saving for that trip and do what I can with Ben. No promises with the last part.*

Thanks, Tara responded. *And don't be too hard on Beth. She looks up to you, and I think being a freshman and a dancer makes her try too hard. I have one suggestion though, see if you can get her to try a different hair style. Get rid of that braid. Lol. Anyway, I hope you find a super cute bikini. Send pics.*

Coral quickly typed, shaking her head. *I'd be more comfortable in a one-piece.*

At least try on a bikini. You'll see I'm right. Then ask yourself what would Tara buy and get that. Gotta go. Love you.

Coral smiled. She didn't know what she'd do without Tara, but sometimes her best friend was full of herself. Tara loved dragging her to boring parties, but Coral wasn't into drinking, smoking, or socializing and preferred to stay home and read.

Aunt Ruby's brand-new green SUV was locked. She leaned against the door and grinned, thinking how strange it would be to see Tara and Ben as a couple. Because their families were friends, she'd been around Ben most of her life and still didn't really know him. Yet Tara claimed to be an expert on him from a distance and asserted that he was deep because he read constantly and was in a band. Tara had a lot of theories about Ben, including one where he would soon go on a world tour with his band and all his songs would be about her. Coral was used to Tara immersing herself in new guys because she'd done it for years.

Beep!

Her aunt unlocked and started the SUV from their condo. Coral quickly climbed in and sank into the black leather driver's seat. Although her mom would have disapproved of the gas guzzler, Coral had to admit it was comfortable, and she liked learning to drive in it.

The mirrors and seat were adjusted by the time Aunt Ruby slid into the passenger's seat with her usual warning as she handed Coral the keys. "Be careful. Watch the other drivers."

Then they headed out to do something they both disliked—shopping. Their first purchase was a travel set to store their shampoo, lotions, toner, and soap, and then her aunt led the way into another store. It was surprising to see shorts, flip-flops, tank tops, and sundresses amid Christmas decorations while the store blasted holiday music. When they couldn't find swimsuits and cover-ups, the sales associate ordered them, promising delivery to their condo before they left. It was evident that they weren't the only people looking for tropical wear for Christmas.

"That should do it. If we need anything else, we can pick it up in Hawaii, right?" Aunt Ruby grinned.

"Right." Coral hopped back into the driver's seat, remembering she'd forgotten to send Tara any pictures. She'd show her later. They left the mall with Christmas music playing on the radio and their packages on the back seat.

***

Neither Ruby nor Coral noticed him following or snapping pictures of them while they shopped. Ned stayed in the shadows, watching. He was enjoying the newest addition to his assignment—the daughter of Emerald and Morgan Dover. It was comfortable watching from the parking lot as they ordered burgers, fries, and chocolate milkshakes. The aunt was much more interested in her phone than her niece.

She's a cold fish.

His stomach grumbled, so he took advantage of this break to eat his packed lunch. He never ate while driving. Too many distractions. Coral gobbled her burger and fries, while Ruby's pace was slow and boring, like her. He snapped a couple more pictures between bites of his tuna sandwich.

How much do you know about your family, Coral? I bet I know more. All you have left of that family is your aunt. No one else on your mother's or father's side. Don't you ever wonder about that, Coral? I would if I were you, especially when it comes to your mother.

He shook his head and then stuffed the rest of the sandwich in his mouth. Coral would be the last of their bloodlines soon.

***

The week flew by, although it wasn't fast enough for Coral with Tara pestering her every time they talked.

"Promise me you'll talk to Ben about me," Tara pleaded.

Coral smiled and nodded. Tara folded her arms and glared at her. "I'll try."

That earned her a grin and a colorful holiday bag shoved into her arms. They had to exchange their presents early since they would be on opposite sides of the country for the holidays.

Coral pulled a yellow tank top with lace and flowers on it out of the snowman gift bag. "I love it." At the bottom of the bag was a small, white box that contained a tiny silver turtle pendant. "Wow, thanks, Tara. This means a lot to me. I'll wear this with my dolphin. Open yours." Her throat tightened as she tried to contain her emotion.

"If I could have found you a bikini, I would have gotten you one. Can't believe you bought a one-piece." Tara shook her head and carefully opened her red snowflake gift bag. "Thank you, Coral. This is awesome. A grizzly wearing a tutu in a pirouette. I know exactly where I'm going to put this one." She gathered Coral into a big hug.

Coral smiled as Tara continued to smother her with affection. The dancing animal figurine was an addition to the growing collection on the shelf above Tara's bed. While Tara had given her an attention-grabbing shirt to encourage her to stand out more, it was the turtle that almost made Coral cry with its connection to her dolphin pendant. The touching moment passed when Tara steered the conversation back to Ben.

"Ben's band, Yellowed Pages, is playing at No Holiday Festival. A bunch of indie bands threw it together for the end of January, and we *have* to go."

"Yeah, well . . . hmmm, sure. It sounds fun." There was no point in arguing with Tara. Coral would go whether she liked it or not.

Honk! Honk!

"There's my mom. I can't wait to take my driving test in February so I don't have to get picked up anymore. Yours is two weeks later, and then we can do what we want, when we want to. Gotta pack. Thanks again, Coral. You're the bestest." Tara rushed out the door.

"Bye—" It was all she managed to get out before the door slammed shut.

She'd miss her in Hawaii. Tara understood her like no one else did and encouraged her to dance it out when something bothered her. Coral usually felt better afterward. They'd become the best dancers at their studio and were in the second year of the advanced dance program at their high school. Dance was what Tara wanted to pursue after graduation. Coral wanted to major in English.

She studied a flower-framed picture on her dresser of the two of them at a recital the previous summer. They were both dressed in flowing blue costumes with shells covering the chest and back. Tara was beautiful—her long blond hair was pulled into a bun, and her prominent brown eyes took up most of her face, making her look exotic.

They were the lead mermaids teasing the sailors, trying to get them to swim with them, which they eventually did when the other mermaids joined them. The glittery seashore set and wavy lights created a breathtaking scene, and Coral had felt oddly at home. The audience were on their feet when they were done. Of course, it was only their relatives, but it was still a moment for all of them, even though later that night, Coral was holding Tara's hair back as she threw up into the toilet after celebrating too much.

Tara conveniently forgot about that part of the night, but after that, she always teased Coral that she was a mermaid. She knew Tara didn't take her dreams seriously, but at least she could talk to her about them without hearing that she was crazy, and Tara never told anyone else. Loyalty, above all else, had been the glue that held their friendship together for so many years.

Coral added the yellow tank top and the new blue swimsuit and white cover-up—which had arrived earlier in the day—to her suitcase, right on top of her mom's book.

"Ready!"

She closed the suitcase, placed it by her bedroom door, and shut off the light. She was overwhelmed with excitement, and sleep was swift in coming.

D. L. Finn

Chapter 3
Heading to Hawaii

Finally it was the last day of school before the holiday break. The half day felt like it would never end. Coral had just turned in her trig test when the bell rang. She made a frantic rush to her locker to deposit the books she wouldn't need in Hawaii.

"I'm *so* glad this day is finally over. It dragged on *forever*!" Tara slammed her locker shut. "Come on, let's get out of here."

They pushed through the crowded halls to the parking lot, where Tara's mother was waiting with a smile.

Tara hugged Coral goodbye. "Sorry we can't drive you home today. We're heading straight to the airport."

"No problem, Tara. I'll miss you." Coral squeezed her best friend.

"I'll miss you too. Don't forget to email me updates from Hawaii. I want to know everything you're doing. Remember, I won't have my cell phone—such a dumb rule—so don't text me, okay? But I will check my email every day. I promise." Tara dashed to her mom's car.

Coral waved as Tara climbed into the driver's side of the blue wagon that she jokingly referred to as the Blue Turtle. A rush of sadness consumed her as her best friend drove away. She scanned the parking lot. Nothing different about it, yet that sense of melancholy continued to weigh heavily upon her. Ben cruised by in his mom's old white Mercedes without a single glance in her direction. Always in his own world. She shook her head. The bus shuddered to a stop in front of her, and she hastily climbed aboard, ready for this vacation.

Amid the normal chaos of the bus, the trip to Hawaii occupied her thoughts. Coral couldn't wait to dive into the ocean to see what was waiting for her. Her dreams had been getting more vivid since learning about the vacation. It was frustrating how close she was to seeing what was in that cave, but she always woke up at that point.

The rest of the day flew by as she and her aunt cleaned the house from top to bottom. After a dinner of pepperoni pizza, it was time for bed.

"Night, Aunt Ruby."

"Sleep fast." Aunt Ruby chuckled. "That alarm will go off before you know it, and we'll be on our way."

Before hopping into bed, Coral rechecked her luggage to make sure she didn't forget anything. Her cell phone buzzed with an email from Tara.

Made it. My roommate is from Lake Tahoe. You'd like her. She wants to meet you when we get home. We start dancing at 8:00 a.m. (which is 5:00 a.m. there), so I had better get some sleep. Let me know when you get to paradise. I'll check tomorrow morning or later, not sure. Miss you.

Coral responded with a simple happy face. She'd type more tomorrow since she doubted Tara would see it until then anyway. She shut off her phone and plugged it in to charge it. Climbing between the red flannel sheets and pulling the comforter over her head, she made a mental note not to forget the charger.

Lying in bed, tossing and turning, she yawned but couldn't sleep. Her mind was spinning, picturing all the things she'd do in Hawaii. The first thing would be to head to the beach and jump into the warm, salty water. She'd swim, snorkel, lie in the sun, and maybe do some sightseeing to take in all the Christmas decorations. There was an aquarium she wanted to see on Maui, and she wanted to take the Hana drive.

But first, on Oahu, she was sure they'd see Pearl Harbor and walk over the sunken *Arizona*, where all those men had died. The thought of the Japanese planes flying over the ships with bullets and bombs sent shivers down her spine. Two waves of attacks had killed 2,403 Americans on December 7, 1941. The United States' entry into World War II was a date she would always remember because December 7 was also her dad's birthday.

She knew she'd feel sad standing over the *Arizona*, not only about the loss of all those people who had served their country like her dad, but for the loss of her parents too. That was the only thing she wasn't looking forward to in Hawaii, yet she knew it was something she needed to face. Her racing mind finally succumbed to sleep around one.

Beep, beep, beep.

It was three in the morning, time to go. She shut off her alarm with an eagerness not present on school days. They rushed out the door fifteen minutes later.

It was an hour-long drive to the Reno airport, with no traffic. Coral pulled her luggage behind her as they maneuvered their way through the terminal. Aunt Ruby pointed to a skier statue covered in holiday poinsettias so bright they made Coral squint. Relief flooded through her when they encountered no long, boring line for security. It was now five thirty, and they were right on schedule.

The next stop was their gate, where they found the Penny family waiting. Beth smiled and patted the empty seat next to her. Ben didn't look up from his e-reader. Coral hugged Mr. Penny and then Mrs. Penny, who had no makeup on, which was unusual for her.

"Sit over here, Coral." Beth waved and then patted the open seat next to her again.

"It's so early." Coral plopped onto the hard seat.

"I didn't get to sleep until after ten last night. I'm so tired!" Beth acted like she had drunk an entire pot of coffee.

"Oh, wow."

"Here." Beth thrust a breakfast sandwich into Coral's hands. "Mom got extras in case you didn't get a chance to eat."

"Thanks. We were going to pick something up after we found you. Thanks, Mrs. Penny."

"You're welcome, dear. We had the driver stop so we could pick up food. Wish you guys had come with us. A driver is always the best way to go, but I understand Ruby and Robert wanting to have a car when they get back so they can go straight to work. You'll ride back with us, Coral, but no need to worry about that now. We have so much fun ahead. Eat up. Won't be many options for food on the plane. I have some snacks in my purse just in case." Mrs. Penny smiled and patted her huge pink bag.

Aunt Ruby held a cup of coffee in one hand and her breakfast sandwich in the other while she studied the phone in her lap. Coral quietly ate as Beth planned their entire trip. There was usually no room to speak when Beth took over a conversation.

Coral turned her focus to Mr. Penny, who kept glancing worriedly at his wife. He held her hand, absentmindedly patting it. When Mrs. Penny smiled at him, it seemed to have a calming effect, but when she looked away again, he returned to studying her with a frown. Something felt wrong about Mrs. Penny. Coral couldn't explain the feeling, but when she had it, she was usually correct.

Maybe she was psychic, like her dad had said her mom was. Coral always knew things. Tara teased her about it, and Mr. Penny didn't believe it, but it only mattered that she did, and even she wasn't sure. Too bad her mom hadn't known not to get on that plane with her dad. Knowing random things didn't help when you didn't understand the important events.

Beth had gone silent and was checking her phone. She snapped a selfie to send to someone. Ben, of course, paid no attention to anyone.

"Take a picture with me. It will document the start of our trip." Beth moved in closer to Coral. "Smile!" Coral smiled as she was directed and heard the click of the phone's camera. "We should take a group shot of everyone. Let's—"

A voice over the intercom interrupted. "Rows one through twenty, please line up for boarding."

Beth sprang out of her seat. "See you on the plane, Coral." In a flash she was at her mother's side, with Ben and Mr. Penny following behind.

Coral and her aunt were at the back of the plane. It would be a while before they were called. As Coral turned her attention to her phone, she felt a chill shoot through her. Worried, she looked around and saw a bearded man staring at the Pennys. He pointed his cell phone at them like he was taking their picture and then turned the camera on her. He caught Coral's eye and gave her a sinister smile with an added wink. Then, stroking his beard, he turned and disappeared around the corner.

***

Ned had gotten all the photographs of Ruby Hyde and Coral Dover he'd been instructed to take. He'd have to be more careful in the future, as young Coral had spotted him. He'd been a little careless this time, but he was confident the beard and sideburns had hidden his face. He had time to kill before he boarded his flight to Oahu. He'd land three hours after them and wouldn't be on duty again until they went to bed. He smiled at a little old lady. She smiled back with absolutely no idea she was smiling at a trained assassin.

***

At six forty-five, the intercom blared that it was their turn to board the plane. Grabbing her backpack, Coral noticed the bearded man had returned. His back was to her, and he was deep in conversation with an older woman. Was he just some crazy guy taking pictures of everyone? He certainly looked crazy by Coral's standards, and, as her mom would say, her warning system had been activated.

Coral almost pointed the man out to her aunt, but their tickets were already being checked. Besides, Aunt Ruby didn't believe in the goosebumps theory as it related to danger. Coral wasn't sure she believed in it wholeheartedly either, but her mom sure had. The old lady who'd been talking with the strange man was now in line, holding a bag of brightly wrapped gifts. The man was walking away—waiting for another flight, maybe? As soon as she got to the door of the plane, all thoughts of him disappeared. It was time to go to Hawaii.

Coral found her window seat, right over the back edge of the right wing. Buckling her seat belt, she watched Aunt Ruby find a spot for her overnight bag and Coral's backpack. Aunt Ruby had placed their new sundresses and the camera in the bag in the event the airline lost their luggage. While the flight attendant instructed the passengers about safety, Coral whipped off a quick email to Tara. *We're taking off now. Will let you know when we land.* She hit send just as they were being told to shut off their cell phones or put them on airplane mode.

"Ready?" Aunt Ruby smiled.

"I am."

This was the first time Coral had been on a plane since her parents had taken her to Disneyland for her fifth birthday. All she remembered from that trip was being tall enough to ride Thunder Mountain and mimicking the "yee-haw" she'd heard on the ride for the rest of the trip. Her parents had laughed every time she said it, so she kept saying it for weeks after. That was another lifetime. She rubbed her temples and watched a man drive away with the empty luggage cart.

After a slow start on the runway, the plane built up speed. Coral's grip on the armrests tightened. Since her parents' disappearance on a plane, flying wasn't as exciting as it used to be. Suddenly the plane was thrust into the air. Aunt Ruby's hand caressed her arm, offering comfort. Coral was glad to have her aunt next to her through this.

When the plane finally leveled out, they were above the clouds and heading closer to the ocean that held the secret of her parents' mysterious disappearance. Coral relaxed and put her headphones on. She quickly found the classic rock. Her dad's favorite Led Zeppelin song, "Kashmir," was playing. He'd always play air guitar to it. Her mom would roll her eyes at his antics while Coral smiled in adoration. Her mom also regularly pointed out that his real guitar was collecting dust in the corner. Coral had always planned on using that guitar someday and wished Aunt Ruby hadn't sold it.

It seemed like they'd just taken flight when they landed in San Francisco. With forty-five minutes between planes, they rushed to their next gate. Soon they were in the air again, overlooking the front of the left wing.

The seat belt sign went off, and her aunt left to find the bathroom. Coral's two hours of sleep finally caught up to her, and she could barely keep her eyes open. Adjusting her neck pillow, she studied the fluffy white clouds that looked as if she could step right off the plane and walk on them. "Dreamboat Annie" by Heart came on next. The lyrics to that song summed up exactly how Coral was feeling at that moment. Before the song ended and her aunt returned, she was fast asleep.

Chapter 4
Smile for the Camera

Coral was abruptly shaken from her dreamless slumber. Was something wrong with the plane? Heart racing and fists clenched, she shot up and frantically looked around. The oxygen masks hadn't dropped, and her aunt looked more relaxed than Coral had ever seen her. A hand gently brushed her arm.

"We're landing now."

Red-faced, Coral relaxed her hands and sank back into her seat. Her aunt had a slight grin as she reached over Coral and opened the window shade.

Coral blinked rapidly as her eyes adjusted to the sun. "I slept for five hours?"

"You did. Look, you can see the island."

Coral slipped on her glasses. "Wow."

Jagged land surrounded by deep blue water—exactly as she'd pictured it. Coral grabbed her phone and snapped some shots. The blues and greens only intensified as the plane flew closer.

A cheerful voice came over the speakers. "Honolulu time is 11:10 a.m., and it's a balmy eighty degrees. Please enjoy your stay during this holiday season. Thank you for choosing Jet Hawaii to fly."

It didn't feel like eleven ten in the morning because it was one ten at home and past lunchtime. Her stomach gurgled loudly, and her aunt handed her a small bag of macadamia nuts in holiday wrapping and a cup of water.

"That's Waikiki Beach over there, and there's Diamond Head—an old volcano." Aunt Ruby pointed as the plane circled down. A white sand beach with specks of people on it was lined by massive hotels, making it look more like a tropical city than a tropical island.

"I can't wait to hit the beach." Coral stuffed the five nuts into her mouth and washed them down with a gulp of water.

"I'm sure Beth and Ben will want to swim right after we eat. However, there's a lot to see on Oahu in only two days. Then we'll be staying on Maui for the remainder of the trip. I did tell you that, right?" Aunt Ruby cast a lingering smile at a movie star–handsome man who was looking back in her direction.

"You did."

Aunt Ruby's cheeks pinkened. "Good. I want you to see as much as you can while we're here. You'll need to listen to Mrs. Penny when I'm working until I can . . . " Her sentence trailed off as she shot another look at the dark-haired man, who winked at her.

"I will."

Aunt Ruby's focus was now on the flirtatious guy. Had this been going on the whole time Coral had slept? Well, if he wasn't a serial killer or anything like that, Coral could get behind her aunt having a man in her life. She put her headphones back on, but there was no music, so she studied the approaching paradise.

The plane landed with a soft thump. When the all-clear was given, the passengers exited quickly into the terminal. Two women wearing matching Hawaiian dresses greeted them. The tropical print on their outfits featured a surfing Santa in shorts and Mr. and Mrs. Claus sitting in a boat being pulled by dolphins.

"Aloha! Welcome to Hawaii." One of the women placed a sweet-smelling lei around her neck.

"Mele Kalikimaka," the other woman added with a huge grin. Coral remembered hearing that phrase in an old Bing Crosby song and knew it meant "Merry Christmas."

Aunt Ruby returned the greeting and started through the crowded terminal. "The Pennys will meet us at the baggage claims area, but it'll take a while for our luggage to come down. Let's grab a snack after we find a restroom."

Soon they were in line at a coffee cart with Hawaiian Christmas carols blaring from a speaker. Tinsel covered the cart, which displayed the same design as the dresses worn by the greeters. It seemed to be a very popular theme. Below the walkway they found an open bench in a peaceful garden to enjoy their treats. Birds landed on the lush greenery while water flowed into ponds filled with koi.

"This cinnamon roll is amazing." Aunt Ruby smacked her lips.

It was so light and fluffy that it melted in Coral's mouth. "It is." It was all she could utter between bites.

Aunt Ruby guzzled her iced mocha down before Coral had even opened her water. The tranquil sound of the fountains was interrupted when her aunt stood up and stretched. "Let's go find the Pennys."

Leading the way through a crowd of people, Aunt Ruby clutched her carry-on bag and Coral's backpack. Coral offered to help but was quickly dismissed with a wave of a hand. "No, I have it."

It was an uncomplicated but long walk through the throng of travelers donned in shorts and smelling of suntan lotion, rushing to get to their next plane or picking up their baggage. The airport was beautiful and full of personality, and the Christmas decorations added to it.

This is going to be the best Christmas ever!

Checking for an email from Tara and finding nothing, she sent her an update. *At the airport. I slept most of the flight. We should be at the hotel soon. Can't wait to jump into the ocean finally. More later.*

They found the Penny family waiting for them at a large baggage claim area decorated with small Christmas trees trimmed in silver-and-gold bows and red flowers.

Aunt Ruby pointed. "Aren't those anthuriums on the tree pretty? We could do that when we get to Maui and—"

"Yoo-hoo!" Mrs. Penny waved to Coral and Aunt Ruby. "We have our luggage already. I can't believe how fast they unloaded it. We'll wait for you over here."

Aunt Ruby waved back. Leaning in to Coral, she whispered, "Beth was disappointed you slept all the way from San Francisco. She came over to visit you, but at least you two will have the entire trip to spend together."

"Yes, the entire trip."

Her aunt didn't hear her as her focus shifted to the mystery man from the plane. Her eyes were glued on him as he grabbed a black bag and walked off. Coral wondered if that was the end of their flirting. Her aunt's attention remained on the man until he disappeared around the corner and out of sight.

She almost told her aunt to go after him and share her cell phone number, but maybe it was for the best that she hadn't.

The sweet scent of the pale yellow-and-pink plumerias in her lei relaxed her. It was like someone had mixed rose, jasmine, gardenia, and citrus together in a glorious Hawaiian blend. She took possession of the backpack and overnight bag with a smile while her aunt retrieved their luggage from the carousel.

"You have everything?" Mrs. Penny asked.

"We do."

"Good. Let's find our ride and get to our hotel." Mrs. Penny led the way.

Coral dutifully followed behind. Mrs. Penny linked her arm with Beth's, chatting loudly about some people who'd been on their flight. "They were so loud and rude."

Beth looked like a parrot, constantly nodding in agreement. Mr. Penny and Aunt Ruby were talking in hushed tones while Ben walked and read simultaneously. Had he ever tripped or fallen doing that? Amazingly, he crossed the street safely, only glancing up once. The group quickly made their way to the hotel van, which was waiting for them.

The driver wore a loud yellow-and-orange floral shirt with, surprisingly, no holiday theme. He held up a sign with the hotel's name on it even though it was written on the side of the van. Coral sighed quietly. Aunt Ruby had no clue that Mrs. Penny, Ben, and Beth made Coral feel uncomfortable. Mr. Penny was the only bright side to that family. Luckily Coral grabbed the seat next to his. There was no room for anyone else.

"This is going to be a great week, Coral. You, Beth, and Ben will have the time of your life. So much to see and do. I hope I get to do some of it with you." Mr. Penny smiled as he looked over at Beth. She eagerly smiled back, but Ben never looked up from his e-reader.

"I can't wait to get to the beach."

Mr. Penny's face reddened. "Yes, the beach. Soon. I'm sure you have some shopping to do first, with Christmas right around the corner?" He glanced across the aisle at Mrs. Penny.

"Naturally, dear. It'll be the best Christmas ever, I promise. But don't worry, Coral, our hotel is right on the beach, and you'll be able to see it from your room. You'll love it." Mrs. Penny winced and adjusted her leg.

Mr. Penny smiled at his wife. When he turned away, his cheerful expression disappeared, revealing a tense grin. It could be simply that Mrs.

Penny hadn't slept well, or . . . Hopefully, there was no "or." It was obvious how much he cared for his family. He'd been there for Coral since her parents went missing and was always willing to listen to her talk about her dreams. It wasn't that long ago that he'd confided to her about his dream during a family barbecue.

"Always the same dream—like you, Coral. It begins with me having a picnic alone in the woods with dark storm clouds rolling in. I stand up and watch until they're right on top of me. Then I run for cover in a dark, damp cave, but I always know I shouldn't be hiding from the storm. It was very confusing to have this same dream every night. You know, it stopped the very day I proposed to Mrs. Penny. Not that I compare her to that storm, but I feel like the bad days, or that storm, were behind me once I committed my life to her." He cleared his throat and continued. "I believe that once you find what you're looking for, your dream will stop too."

Mr. Penny also encouraged her to talk about her parents, especially her dad. He was careful not to speak about her parents or the dream in front of anyone else, and he was also close-lipped about what they had been doing when their plane disappeared. Whenever she asked, he always changed the subject with a sad smile.

Coral jumped when the hotel van driver finished loading their luggage and closed the door with a loud bang.

"Why don't you and Beth sit together? She can fill you in on all the sights."

"Oh, I don't want to bother her."

"Bother her? Why, she's been so excited to spend this vacation with you! Plus, I have a wife who needs some tending to." He winked at his wife and stood up.

"Beth, honey. Come sit next to Coral so I can be next to your mom."

"Okay, Dad." Beth jumped up.

"Coral was hoping you'd point out some of the scenery along the way. I'm sure you remember some of it, don't you?"

Beth plopped down next to Coral right as the stranger from the airplane, who'd been exchanging coy glances with Aunt Ruby, banged on the door. The driver sighed as he opened it and greeted the man but made no offer to help him with his luggage, which invoked a quick scowl. The man put his suitcase next to Aunt Ruby's bag on the rack and then took a seat next to her.

So he's staying at our hotel too? That's certainly a coincidence.

Beth smoothed her yellow shorts, even though there were no wrinkles. A single glance and Beth would burst into chatter, so instead, Coral directed her full attention to the parking lot. There was a lady with black hair in a ponytail, wearing a long, colorful Hawaiian dress, who was taking pictures of the van, and she seemed to be focusing on Aunt Ruby. It was similar to what the man in Reno had done. Then the lady turned her camera on Coral and Beth. They weren't celebrities—why would people randomly take pictures of them?

The woman noted Coral's attention and scurried away, never looking back. She disappeared around the corner as the van pulled away and headed out of the airport. Once again, goosebumps crawled up Coral's arms—and not from the cold air flowing from the wide-open vents. Perhaps the lady worked for the company that ran the van service for the hotel? Was she keeping track of their customers or taking photographs to sell them later? None of these seemed plausible. Spotting not one but two people taking pictures of them in one day seemed very peculiar.

***

Kini watched the van drive away. She'd gotten the pictures of Coral Dover and Ruby Hyde and wondered why these ordinary-looking people were of so much interest to her clients. Unfortunately, that information wasn't necessary to do her job effectively. She dutifully texted the pictures to the number provided and headed to her car.

She fretted over Coral spotting her, although it was doubtful the young woman would figure out that someone had hired people to follow her. No, Coral would think she was a fellow tourist taking pictures. If seen again, she'd add in a selfie for realism. The person that concerned her the most was the ex-general, Robert Penny, although he seemed too distracted by his wife to notice they were being shadowed.

Kini threw her old white Honda into gear and headed out of the airport. It was going to be a long day, and their destination was known. There was enough time to stop and grab a cup of coffee and maybe an energy bar to get her through it. A loud sigh escaped her as she clicked on her turn signal. The instructions had been very clear: keep these people in sight at all times. That seemed overkill with this group, but like her mother used to say, "A'ole pilikia—no problem, no trouble."

A lump formed in her throat as she squeezed into a space at the quick mart. She missed her mom, but some days she wished she'd never followed her to the islands after she retired. Her mother had loved being home again. It had certainly helped that she had just enough money to survive until she died in the nursing home. Money wasn't as easy to come by for Kini. Some days she thought about moving back to California, but she'd become too used to island living. It took some extra jobs to make ends meet, and not all of them were legal.

Kini walked out of the store, snacks in hand. Next time, she'd bring some wine to make the days more interesting.

***

Aunt Ruby pretended to take in the scenery outside her window while intentionally ignoring the man sitting next to her. She kept smoothing the same hairs back from her flushed cheeks until the man leaned over and pointed. Aunt Ruby giggled, opening the door for their conversation.

Beth's eyes were locked on Coral. "You don't have to tell me about everything we see. It's all right."

Beth let out a gush of air. "Oh, good. I don't remember all the history and other stuff Dad told me about before. But there are so many fun things to do here. Last time we all got matching Hawaiian outfits. Maybe we could match this time?"

Coral nodded. Maybe she should have let Beth tell her about the sights after all.

Beth grinned. "You'll love the mall. It's Mom's favorite place to go. I bet it will be pretty this time of year with all the holiday decorations."

Before she could stop it, a frown formed on Coral's face, prompting Beth to add, "Maybe I can talk her out of going to the mall."

"Could you?" Coral broke into a genuine smile.

Beth paused for a moment, knitting her brows together. "I'll try, but shopping is one of her favorite things to do, especially around Christmas. I think you might like it. Mom knows all the good places to shop. Anyway, we must stop at Waimea Falls. It's so pretty. We never go without seeing Pearl Harbor. You do remember me mentioning how my great-uncle was killed at Pearl Harbor?"

She nodded. Beth found that story exciting, but it only made Coral depressed.

"Well, then we go on to the next island. We *have* to do the Hana drive, with all those waterfalls and pools. Maui has some great shopping . . . " Beth continued talking about shopping even though Coral had made it clear shopping didn't interest her, so she tuned her out, remembering to nod here and there.

Finally, after some thick traffic, the van exited the freeway and headed toward Waikiki Beach and their hotel.

Chapter 5
Checking In

The massive pink hotel faced the beach like a flower opening to the sun. The lobby, bathed in a gentle vanilla shade with tropical bird murals and matching couches, suggested a peaceful atmosphere, but the holiday decorations caught Coral's eye. A large green tree filled with beach-themed ornaments was the centerpiece. Carefully wrapped presents with glittery fake crabs climbing around them adorned the bottom of the tree. It didn't surprise Coral that the large plastic Santa standing next to the tree was wearing an unbuttoned Hawaiian shirt and loud swim trunks. Barefoot and holding a surfboard, he was making the shaka, or hang loose, sign—his pinky and thumb up and the rest of his fingers tucked into his hand.

While Mr. Penny and Aunt Ruby checked them in, Mrs. Penny and Beth were in deep conversation about shopping. A quick scan of the room showed no one was taking pictures of them.

Soon Mr. Penny and Aunt Ruby came back with the room keys, minus their luggage.

"I know we missed lunch, and it's almost dinner time at home. Do you want to eat now or wait?" Mr. Penny asked.

Eat now was the consensus. Coral ate a juicy cheeseburger and crispy curly fries with a sweet chunk of pineapple while admiring people in the deep blue water off the packed beach. She couldn't wait to join them.

Aunt Ruby cleared her throat, pulling Coral's attention back to the table. Ben looked up for a moment as he stuffed the rest of his burger in his mouth and gave her a slight grin. Coral raised an eyebrow back.

"Are you tired?"

Coral shook her head. "No. Why?"

"Well, Beth's been telling you about the hula lessons you can take at the hotel. I thought maybe you were too tired to answer." Aunt Ruby added a pinched look to her face.

Mr. Penny spoke up. "Oh, I'm sure she was watching the waves. They have the same effect on me. Coral was just telling me back at the airport how much she was looking forward to all the stuff planned for her, right?"

Coral nodded quickly as heat flushed her cheeks. "Oh, of course. I can't wait. I was watching those surfers over there. It looks fun, doesn't it?"

"Yes, fun." Beth's tone didn't match her words. Her face perked up. "What about scuba diving? We had so much fun last year doing that on the Big Island. Maybe we could teach them."

Mrs. Penny elegantly dabbed her mouth, carefully folded her napkin, and gently shook her head. "No time for surfing, and scuba lessons are time-consuming. We're certified to dive, remember? We can probably squeeze in some snorkeling or hula lessons over on Maui, though. I think you'll enjoy that, Coral. Should we get started?"

"Yes, sounds fun."

Mr. Penny looked over at Aunt Ruby. "Ruby and I have some work we need to attend to. We'll meet you for dinner."

"Can you make the sunset around six?" Mrs. Penny asked.

"Of course—I'd hate to miss one with you." He kissed her cheek.

Coral stood up. "Should I get my swimsuit?"

"We won't be needing swimsuits where we're going. Maybe later. I think we should start this vacation right with a shopping trip. Have to look like the Hawaiians, I say." Mrs. Penny smiled at Beth as she nodded in agreement.

So much for talking her mother out of shopping.

"Be good." Aunt Ruby slipped $40 into Coral's palm.

Coral wasn't sure if the taxi ride to go shopping or the actual buying of the matching clothes would be the day's low point. The trip from the airport had been cool and comfortable. This taxi-van had no air-conditioning, and it was humid and hot. The open windows barely helped. To make the short ride even more unbearable, the driver told the story of how King Kamehameha unified all the Hawaiian Islands and was the last king after the Spanish came—which Coral already knew.

When they pulled up to Ala Moana Mall, Mrs. Penny and Beth were off. Beth had not only *not* talked her mom out of shopping, but she looked just as excited as her mom to be there. Beth's worship of Coral didn't apply when it came to shopping.

"These T-shirts will be perfect for you and Ruby."

They weren't bad—blue, purple, and orange tropical flowers. "Perfect, thanks." Coral tried to sound excited.

"Oh, look at this, will you, Beth? You and Coral can match—wait, so can Ben!"

This went on for the next hour, with every matching combination covered. They kept passing by a huge tree sitting atop a present. Coral was surprised to see a traditional Santa there and worried Mrs. Penny would want them to take a picture with him, but surprisingly, she didn't even give Santa a passing look.

When it seemed like they were finally done, they moved on to a shop that carried Hawaiian collectibles. It was here that Coral spent most of her money, buying a Hawaiian good-luck statue and a Waikiki sunset magnet for the fridge to give to her aunt for Christmas. She also purchased some postcards, a glitter pen, a journal, and some sour watermelon candy for Beth and Ben. Ben responded to his gift with a huge grin and immediately ate it, but Beth tucked hers away into the pocket of her shorts.

Then they entered a rather expensive jewelry shop. Before Coral could stop herself, she let out a huge sigh. She heard Ben chuckle behind her, but luckily Mrs. Penny and Beth didn't hear it.

Then Coral saw it. "My necklace!"

"Yes, it is," Mrs. Penny said. "Here are a pair of earrings to go with it—and a bracelet. What do you think?"

"Oh, I don't know. It's pretty expensive here."

Mrs. Penny held up her hand. "Oh, don't worry about the money. Your aunt texted me. She was worried she didn't give you enough spending money and said to let you get anything you wanted. She said she'd pay me back, but it's not necessary. I enjoy doing this, especially at Christmas. They even have a turtle charm that you can add to the dolphin bracelet to match that turtle your friend gave you. Let's just wrap it up and consider it a Christmas present from me."

"Thank you, but—" Coral began but was cut off by Mrs. Penny shaking her head.

"No buts! Beth is getting some jewelry too. She found a darling whale set. Did she show you? I guess I'm getting Christmas presents for her too, but—" Mrs. Penny's face went pale as she grabbed the counter before plopping down in a lounge chair in the beach display nearest her.

Coral rushed to her side, kneeling next to her. "Are you okay?"

"Oh, fine, dear. I moved my head too fast. You know how it is after a long plane flight. Let's make our purchases and get out of here, kids." She quickly rose from the chair, still looking a little pale, and barreled up to the counter with her final purchases, dragging her other bags behind her.

Concern washed over Ben's face. Sighing, he approached his mom from behind, relieving her of all her bags and her purse. Mrs. Penny started to protest but smiled fondly at him instead. He went back to reading while she made her final purchases.

Coral studied her silver dolphin necklace, which now included the silver turtle from Tara, and wondered where her parents had bought it. They hadn't been to Hawaii yet, so maybe they'd found it in Reno or online, like Tara. Coral sighed. She'd probably never know much about her most treasured possession, but the necklace made her feel close to her parents.

"We covered a lot of ground in the last hour and a half. I'm done for today."

Beth smiled at Coral timidly. "It's so hot. Do you think we could get ice cream?"

"That's a fine idea. Let's grab a taxi back to the hotel, and we can get some ice cream there. Hopefully, this next taxi will have air-conditioning. I'm getting too old for this heat. Let's hurry, kids. I see a taxi out front."

The ride back to the hotel was shorter and more pleasant than the one before. Luckily, the air-conditioned taxi was driven by someone uninterested in giving them island history. Finally seated at their hotel with an ocean view, Mrs. Penny's iced cappuccino put a smile on her face while Beth, Ben, and Coral enjoyed waffle cones stuffed with pineapple ice cream. Coral was quickly becoming a fan of everything pineapple. The combination of sweet and tart in a crunchy cone was just what was needed after that shopping trip.

"Look at the time. It's after five! If you want to swim, we'd better hurry up. Boy, did this day fly by! If I had realized how late it was, I think I'd have held off on your ice cream treats, but it's vacation, so maybe it's not so bad to eat your dessert first," Mrs. Penny rattled on as everyone got on the elevator. She looked through the bags Ben was holding and handed Coral her things to take back to her room. "We did well today!" She beamed at Beth, who returned the smile.

It appeared that shopping was more than a hobby. It felt like an Olympic event. They deserved a gold medal for today. Coral choked back a laugh thinking of Mrs. Penny and Beth standing at the podium having medals placed around their necks. At least now she understood why Ben read all the time.

Mrs. Penny had been generous to her with new earrings, a bracelet, and the clothes. Without even participating Ben ended up with a collection of things too. He bought a book about Hawaiian myths, information she would pass on to Tara. Her best friend would soon develop an interest in mythology—if she could find something about it on YouTube.

"Will you be okay in your room? Do you want me to check it first?" Mrs. Penny asked as Coral unlocked the room she would share with Aunt Ruby, next door to Mr. and Mrs. Penny's.

"I'm fine. I'll call if I need anything."

"Okay. Get your suit on and grab a towel if you have one. If you don't, I have an extra. We'll meet you back in the café in about ten minutes." She disappeared into their room without waiting for Coral's response.

D. L. Finn

Chapter 6
Swimming in the Ocean

The blue-and-green tropical room was cozy, with two double beds, a TV, desk, microwave, coffeemaker, and Coral's favorite part—a balcony. The view pulled her attention to the beach packed with tourists. People like her had flown from all parts of the world to swim in the warm Pacific Ocean.

Off to her left was Diamond Head, jutting straight up into the tropical landscape. It was a spectacular view, but it was the azure water that called to her. It expanded beyond her imagination, the gentle waves inviting her to dive in. A floating platform close to shore had a mother and two sons perched on it. Soon it would be her turn. Coral grinned as she left the amazing scene. She set her luggage on a stand, removed her fragrant lei, and pulled on her swimsuit.

Blue and sparkly, it reminded her of the mermaid dance costume. The sides and back were cut more daringly than she was used to, but it flattered her figure. Brushing her long wavy, brown hair, she was glad Tara had talked her out of cutting it into a chin-length bob last summer. She liked the way it looked flowing down her back.

The dolphin beach towel, her cover-up, cell phone, and room key were all stuffed into the blue beach bag. There was an open elevator, and she found Beth waiting when she stepped out.

"That's super cute on you, Coral."

"Thanks, I like yours too. The style suits you," Coral responded, not mentioning their swimsuits were the same design.

"I was thinking the same about yours."

As soon as they reached the shoreline, Beth and Coral threw down their towels next to Ben's backpack. While adjusting her bathing suit, she caught Ben's half grin and hid her blush by turning away and tucking her glasses into her bag.

"See you in the water." Coral took off across the warm, soft sand.

A look behind her showed a shirtless Ben. He was no longer the tall, skinny boy she remembered. He removed his glasses, put them in his backpack, and started toward the water's edge.

"Come on!" Beth called.

Coral tore her gaze away from Ben and maneuvered through the crowd. She dove right into the warm sea while Ben stood knee deep in the water. Opening her eyes underwater, she saw legs all around her and, off to the left, a group of rocks. She'd hoped to see fish or a turtle, but there was nothing except humans as far as her eyes could see, and they couldn't see all that well. Next shopping trip, she'd get a mask. Knowing the Pennys, that'd be soon.

It was free and peaceful in the quiet waves, but a small part of her wished for the ability to breathe underwater. Then she could swim out past everyone to see what was out there hidden under all the blue. Instead, her lungs needed air. Surfacing, she rubbed and blinked her eyes to clear them.

Aunt Ruby and Mr. Penny had arrived, and her aunt was sitting next to someone on a towel. Without her glasses it was hard to make out who it was, but she could pick out her aunt's laugh. Was it the same man she'd met on the plane or someone new?

"Come on, you two. I'll meet you on the platform." Beth swam ahead.

"Meet you there," Ben called from behind her.

Coral put all her effort into getting to the platform. It was a surprise to find Beth already lying quietly in the departing sun. She joined her and closed her eyes. There was a thump that swayed them like a rocking chair as Ben climbed on. She focused on the yelling and splashing as the platform continued its soothing motion. A relaxed sigh escaped her. She peeked to make sure no one had heard. Beth and Ben looked serene, like they were sleeping. Her eyes stopped on Ben's shoulders.

When did they get so big?

Tara wouldn't have missed that detail. She wished her friend was here with her. But company aside, it was time to embrace the perfect moment:

relaxing on the wooden platform, soaking in paradise. She dozed off and awoke with a shiver.

The sun was beginning to set, taking with it the warming rays. Coral shot up. "Race you back to shore." She jumped into the blue water with a big splash and swam fast. The water exploded again, and Beth was close behind.

The water was cloudy and dark, and it was hard to see anything. She surfaced, expecting to see Beth next to her, but it was Ben. Beth was right behind them.

"Kids!" Mrs. Penny called. "I have your towels. You'd better get out now and dry off before you catch a cold. We'll watch the sunset from here."

They emerged from the gentle waves. Coral hated leaving, but Mrs. Penny was right. It was time to watch the sunset. She sank into the warm sand, bundled in her towel, and nestled her glasses back atop her nose. The sky took on the orange and red hues of fall.

The sun dove below the ocean in a fiery ball. There was a hushed respect for the beauty of the sky against the lingering clouds framed by palm trees. Coral knew she would never forget this sight. She snapped a photo before the sun disappeared completely. It didn't capture exactly what she saw in front of her, but it was close.

Still no message from Tara. Coral updated her again.

You must be super busy. I had to shop all day with the Pennys. Yeah, I hated every minute of it. We swam after dinner, but only for a bit. I haven't gotten a picture of Ben for you yet. Maybe you were right about him—he might not be too bad after all. By the way, he bought a book on Hawaiian mythology. I'll keep you updated. Email me back soon. Miss you.

Coral attached the sunset picture because she noticed it had part of Ben's arm and head in it.

That should tease her a little.

"You kids warm?" Mrs. Penny asked.

Ben couldn't stay away from his reading for too long, and Beth was on her phone. Without lifting their eyes, they all nodded.

"Good. I'll take you guys up to get changed, and then we can enjoy dinner." Mrs. Penny glanced over at Mr. Penny and Aunt Ruby.

Coral ran her fingers through her wet hair. "I'm okay. I have my cover-up."

"Don't be silly," Mrs. Penny replied. "You don't want to walk around in a wet suit and a cover-up at dinner."

"I don't mind."

Aunt Ruby intervened. "Well, I do."

"Yes, it will only take a moment." Mr. Penny took his wife's hand to help her up.

Beth and Ben did not disagree with their mother. As soon as they turned to leave, the woman from the airport appeared behind them, taking their picture again. Coral met her eyes, and the woman awkwardly turned her phone on herself, pretending to take a selfie. She glanced slyly in Coral's direction and then darted away.

Coral shook her head. "That's strange."

"What is?" Aunt Ruby came up behind Coral.

"When we were at the Reno airport, a bearded man was taking pictures of all of us. When we got to Hawaii, I noticed a woman in a muumuu taking pictures of us when we were sitting in the van. Just now, that same woman was taking pictures of us again." Coral finished loud enough for the whole group to hear.

Mrs. Penny glanced at her husband. "Well, isn't that odd?"

"I doubt it's the same person." Aunt Ruby swept her hand out. "Look around. Everyone is taking pictures."

"Yes, it would be odd if that were the case." Mr. Penny threw a look over the crowd.

"Maybe we look famous," Beth chimed in.

Ben remained silent, but a slow frown crept across his brows.

"I'm positive it was the same person. When she saw me looking at her, she even pretended to be taking selfies." A quiver shot through Coral's body, and she pulled the towel around her even tighter. It was a warning.

"See, that's what I was worried about. You're cold, Coral. Let's get you kids changed."

"I'm sure there's a logical explanation, Coral. Perhaps she was only taking pictures of herself and you misinterpreted it." Mr. Penny started to walk, leading the group.

Coral frowned. If anyone took pictures of them again, she'd turn the tables—pull out her phone and take snapshots of them. Everyone was acting like she was crazy or imagining what she'd seen. She didn't care. She knew.

"Come on, Coral!" Aunt Ruby called.

"I'm coming." Coral ran after the group.

After everyone changed into their new outfits, they met back in the lobby and headed to the restaurant, where a waiter immediately took their orders. Coral ordered the crab Louie special, as everyone else did. Soon she was savoring the best salad she'd ever had, loaded with succulent crab, eggs, asparagus, and cheese. She absorbed the sound of the waves crashing on the pale, sandy beach right below their table. Each impulse brought something new, so nothing was ever the same on the shore or beneath its waters. The ocean could deposit a beautiful seashell or a stinging jellyfish.

Below the surface swam fish, turtles, dolphins, and sharks, and those were exactly what she wanted in her life right now. She was tired of her empty life where everything was the same as the day before, where the only promise of happiness rested in the same dream every night. Convinced she'd find the answers she so desperately sought here, in the waters of Hawaii, she pushed away her empty plate while the conversation around her continued.

"Coral!" This was the second time Aunt Ruby had interrupted Coral's thoughts while on their vacation.

"Uh, yes?" Coral tore her gaze away from the ocean.

"Mr. Penny was just commenting on how your dress matches your eyes."

"Well, that, and I was also pointing out that I was having dinner with the most beautiful women on this island."

"Thank you."

"Dear, you did a fine job shopping today. Everyone looks great." He rubbed his wife's hand.

"Yes, I think they do. Thank you!" Mrs. Penny beamed, and the dullness from earlier was gone from her face.

"It was very nice of you to do this for us." Aunt Ruby nodded gratefully.

"No problem, Ruby. You know how I enjoy shopping and gifting others." Mrs. Penny smiled.

"Ready for our after-dinner walk?" Mr. Penny stood up and helped Mrs. Penny. Coral reluctantly left the amazing view.

D. L. Finn

Chapter 7
Photos and Dessert

The hotel lobby sparkled with bright lights. People rushed past them, headed in all directions. Ben tapped Coral's shoulder and nodded toward a woman in a loud dress wearing sunglasses she didn't need and a hat. It was her, with her cell phone pointed at them. Coral fumbled to pull her cell phone out of her bag, but the lady in the muumuu was exiting the lobby before she could get it out. She glanced at Ben, but his eyes were glued to the spot where the lady had been.

He leaned in. "I saw her too, taking pictures of us here and at the airport, but I didn't see the guy in Reno. Sorry. She wasn't taking selfies, and her phone was trained on us. Next time, we'll get that shot of her."

A partner in figuring out this mystery! "I'm going to keep my cell phone ready."

"Me too." Ben nodded.

Beth shot her brother a knowing look that he ignored, and then she smiled at Coral. She didn't need Beth's matchmaking attempts this vacation, unless they were on Tara's behalf.

Coral remembered the first time Tara had shared that she liked Ben. "You're kidding, right?"

Tara laughed. "I'm not. There's something special about him, you know?"

"No, I don't know," Coral had all but shouted.

But now she was changing her mind about him—as a person, not about him being Tara's new boyfriend. "I'll pull him out of his shell, just like I

41

did with you. He won't care about reading all the time when he has me as his girlfriend."

She smiled at the memory and smoothed back her hair, ready for their evening walk.

"Ready?" Mr. Penny asked, looking at his wife.

"Do you mind if we use the ladies' room first?"

"Of course not. I think I'll take advantage of it too."

"Coming, Coral?" Beth asked.

"I'm fine. I'll wait here."

Soon Coral was sitting alone. She sank into the tropical bird–print couch, studying surfing Santa. A memory of her parents hit her. She had overheard her dad ask her mom if she believed in Santa.

"Why not? Just because we can't see him doesn't make him any less factual," her mom replied.

Coral was seven at that time, and she wondered why her dad would ask such a question, but she loved her mom's response. Her dad didn't think the way her mom did, but his love for her was very real—even a child could see that. Coral had been lucky in her parents. They had given her unconditional love and taught her to trust herself.

She exhaled loudly and tore her eyes away from the holiday display. A single tear ran down her cheek, so she removed her silver-rimmed glasses and wiped away her sadness. On a whim she added some pink lipstick.

She wasn't high maintenance like Tara, and she was okay with being plain, or—as Tara's popular friend called her—cute. Katy Long spoke to Coral directly for the first and only time during gym class.

"Coral, you're kind of cute without makeup. A little makeup, and you'd be pretty." She backed up the comment with a grin, and Coral had offered a small, forced smile in return. Then Katy looked pointedly over at a girl sitting by herself. "Some people, no matter how much makeup they put on, it won't help. They'll always be ugly."

Katy shook her head and pranced off. Her comment had been meant for that poor girl, and Coral immediately felt the girl's pain. She was overweight and wearing too much makeup but certainly not ugly. The girl's face was contorted like she was going to cry.

"She's wrong." Coral attempted to comfort the girl.

She shook her head, pushed past Coral, and disappeared without a word into the locker room.

Coral learned later that the girl's name was Belle, and her efforts to befriend her were rejected. Within two weeks Belle transferred to another school. Coral didn't forget Belle and the lesson of what a few simple words could do to a person and how one could be pretty on the outside and ugly on the inside. She hated how mean people could be to each other.

Aunt Ruby startled Coral out of her musings. "Ready?"

"I am."

Her aunt had tucked a flower above her ear and let her hair down. She wore red lipstick and green eyeshadow along with her usual mascara. The dress Mrs. Penny had bought her accentuated her figure perfectly.

"The man I met on the plane—Aaron—he'll be joining us for our walk tonight. He wants to meet me by the bar, and we'll come over so he can formally meet everyone. He's excited to meet you, Coral." She rushed off.

Coral wasn't so sure she was excited to meet him, though.

Beep beep.

An email from Tara.

Oh! I am jealous. What a beautiful sunset, and I noticed you got part of Ben in the picture. Yeah, he is super cute, and the best part is, he doesn't know it yet. I'm having a great time. We dance from the minute we get up until dinnertime. Then we just hang out. You'll like Haley. She reminds me of you. I must go—bedtime here. I will write more later and give you a full update. Miss you!

Coral glanced at the bathroom doors, wondering what was taking everyone so long, and went to check. She ran smack into Beth exiting.

"Oh! Sorry. I'll wait for you by the door."

"Okay."

Coral washed her hands and checked her hair. In the mirror she could see that Mrs. Penny's stall door was ajar. She watched her open a prescription bottle and wash down several pills with a bottle of water. Then she cradled her head in her hands.

The main bathroom door flung open, and Beth came back in.

"I forgot my brush!"

Mrs. Penny stood up, smiling quickly, and exited the stall like nothing was wrong.

Is she sick or addicted to something? The way Mr. Penny treated her so delicately made Coral lean toward illness.

Mrs. Penny looked surprised but recovered quickly with a smile. "Oh, Coral. I didn't hear you come in."

Beth grabbed her pink brush. "I love that lipstick color on you. It makes your eyes pop!"

"Thanks." Coral tore her gaze off of Mrs. Penny.

They exited the restroom together, and they ran into Mr. Penny and Ben.

"I'm surrounded by beauty," Mr. Penny said.

Coral held back a smile as she thanked him.

His flashy new Hawaiian shirt took attention off his round face and thinning hair. He was the only person who could make a shirt like that look dignified.

"Thank you." Mrs. Penny had added a flower to her hair, just like Aunt Ruby, and offered one to Beth, who quickly tucked it into the top of her braid, and Coral, who declined.

"Let's go meet Ruby's new fella."

Over at the bar, Aunt Ruby and her new friend were standing extremely close to each other. Her aunt was blushing when they approached them. The goosebumps ran up her back again. Was that lady lurking somewhere, taking their pictures? Coral scanned the room with her cell phone ready but didn't see her. Then she turned her attention to Aunt Ruby's new friend.

"Here's—" Aunt Ruby began.

The stranger interrupted. "I apologize for not introducing myself earlier. I admit to just wanting her to myself on the beach, but it must have seemed rude. I've heard so much about all of you. My name is Aaron Harvey, and would you believe we only live an hour apart and I do business with the company you work for?" Aaron extended a hand to Mr. Penny.

Grasping his hand firmly, Mr. Penny looked Aaron squarely in the eye to size him up. "I understand. Nice to meet you, Aaron. My name is Robert. This is my wife, Sarah; my son, Ben; my daughter, Beth; and Ruby's niece, Coral."

"A pleasure to meet you all." Aaron turned to shake everyone's hand. When he got to Coral, he didn't let go of her hand as quickly as he had everyone else's. A huge smile slowly crept across his face as his eyes widened. "I can't wait to get to know you better. Your aunt is very proud of you."

"Thank you."

Why would Aunt Ruby be discussing her with this stranger so quickly? They'd just met.

"Ruby tells me you're going for a walk. How do you feel about ice cream? I know an ice cream parlor down the street that serves the best desserts in the area." Aaron finally let go of Coral's hand and latched on to Aunt Ruby's possessively.

"Sounds good! Lead the way." Mr. Penny held his arm out, allowing Aaron to guide them.

The walk was uneventful. Coral walked behind her aunt and Aaron the whole way, and not once did he let go of her hand. Beth was explaining what they would be doing the next day.

Stop trying so hard.

It would crush Beth if she said that out loud. Mrs. Penny had booked a tour for them. Beth hoped they would stop at lots of places along the way because there were so many things she thought Coral should see.

Ben was quiet behind them, probably reading again. What did he read, fiction, nonfiction? Adventure stories or books on how to build boats? She preferred good fantasy stories filled with lots of adventure and left nonfiction for school reading. Beth read those cheesy love stories all the time, but Coral could never get through an entire romance. The stories were too fake, and things like that would never happen to someone like her.

They entered a brightly lit pink and white ice cream parlor. Surf's Swirls had a large silver tree covered in red flowers, just like the one at the airport. Tinsel lined the walls.

"A large banana split with an extra cherry," Mr. Penny said. "That's plenty for the two of us."

"Yes, it is." Mrs. Penny stumbled.

Mr. Penny's face paled as he grabbed her to prevent her from falling. "You're worn out, Sarah. Please find a table to sit and relax. I'll bring the sundae to you."

"You worry too much." She wandered off to find a table.

"What would you like? Would you like to share something too?" Aaron asked Aunt Ruby.

"I'd love to share something. You pick. I like being surprised." She smiled.

"Okay. I'll get my favorite. I'm sure you'll like it. Why don't you go sit with Sarah and keep her company?" Aaron suggested, kissing her cheek.

Aunt Ruby floated over to the table Mrs. Penny had found and melted into a seat.

"Kids? What would you like?" Mr. Penny asked.

Beth spoke up first while Coral was still studying the menu. "I'd like a pineapple milkshake, please. I'll meet you at the table, Coral."

"Okay. Maybe Ben should go next—I'm still deciding."

"I'll have the Sun in the Car, with extra chocolate, please." Ben made his way to the table.

A Sun in the Car was a caramel-and-chocolate sundae—what she and Tara would have ordered back home. She'd try something new.

"A Hawaiian sundae, please."

When it was time to pay, she watched Mr. Penny pull out his wallet. Aaron had made no offer, not even for himself and Aunt Ruby.

"I'll bring your order to you when it's up," the server smiled. "Please make yourselves comfortable. Mahalo."

As soon as Mr. Penny sat next to Mrs. Penny, Aaron sank down next to Aunt Ruby, patting the open seat next to him.

"Please, sit next to me. I'd like to get to know you better." He pulled out the chair for Coral. Aunt Ruby beamed as she sat down.

"Thank you."

The Pennys were deep in conversation, even Ben. His wavy brown hair was messy, which made him look, well, cute. Aunt Ruby was smiling at Aaron, but his attention was on Coral.

"Your aunt tells me you're in your second year of high school. How do you like it?" he asked, shooting Aunt Ruby a quick smile.

"It's okay, I guess." Coral suspected he wasn't listening.

"Yes. I hear you're good at school and that you get good grades. That's important, you know. We should all use the minds we were given, right, Ruby?" Aaron stroked her aunt's cheek.

"Oh yes, Aaron. She does very well."

Aaron's deep brown eyes seemed to peer into her soul. "Do you like to swim, Coral?"

"Swim? Yes, I enjoy swimming." Coral held back a frown.

"Good, good. It's important to know how to swim, you know."

He had a way about him that made you want to trust him, yet Coral didn't. She was confused by his questions, but maybe he just didn't know how to talk to teenage girls.

"Do you want to be a scientist like your mom was? I know she had you when she started college. Must have rubbed off on you. And your aunt tells me she believed in magic—do you?" His gaze was more intense now, as if he wanted to know more than he was asking.

"Um." Coral adjusted her dress and pushed her hair back. Ben was watching her. She met his gaze as he frowned. "I think I'd like to be a teacher, but I'm not sure. As for magic, I'd like to believe there's more out there than I can see."

Aaron clapped his hands together, startling Coral. "I'm glad you realize that. You'd make a fine teacher someday—once you see what's out there, of course. I hear you dance too, and that it would take my breath away, or so your aunt tells me. I can't wait to see you at your next show. Follow your dreams, as they say, and never give up on them."

Mr. Penny frowned at Aaron, his brow raised. Ben's full attention was now on Aaron too, his expression the same as his dad's.

"So true, Aaron. They can come true." Aunt Ruby grinned like a schoolgirl.

"Yes, they can. Don't forget that, Coral. Follow through on your dreams."

At that moment their ice cream arrived. Aaron lost interest in Coral, giving her a chance to eat in peace while he spoon-fed her giggling aunt. It was almost as if he knew about her dreams. She planned to keep an eye on him, especially to make sure her aunt didn't get hurt. He was strange and creepy.

Coral sighed and studied her disappearing pineapple ice cream sundae. It was more than she was used to eating and loaded with fresh pineapples, topped off with whipped cream and a cherry. She was halfway through when a chill went through her body. Aaron was watching her with a half smile. He winked at her and went back to feeding her aunt.

Aaron added a heaviness to the table that weighed down the vacation cheer that had flowed freely at dinner.

Beth pushed away the empty glass. "How was your sundae? It looked so good. My milkshake was perfect. You should try it next time, seriously."

"It was great. Yeah, I'll try it next time, for sure." Coral finished the last two bites.

Ben tossed his napkin into the empty bowl. "I enjoyed mine too."

"You always get the same sundae. Of course you liked it." Beth twisted her mouth and rolled her eyes.

"And I figured you figured that."

"That was perfect." Mrs. Penny dabbed the corners of her mouth with a pink-and-white napkin.

"Yes, it was good. Thanks for suggesting this place to us, Aaron." Mr. Penny carefully wiped his mouth.

"My pleasure," Aaron replied. "Everyone done? It will be nice to stroll back to the hotel and maybe sit on the beach for a bit."

"Sounds like a perfect idea." Aunt Ruby grinned.

"Let's go."

Chapter 8
Look Both Ways before You Cross the Street

They stepped into the tropical night. The streetlights emitted a subdued glow, and the tourist shops were all closed. Coral heard a loud click as the woman in Surf's Swirls locked the door behind them.

"Look, Ruby." Aaron pointed to a jewelry store.

"Oh, let's go look."

He guided Aunt Ruby much like a father helping his child cross the street. Coral held back an eye roll and stepped into the road, noting distant headlights off to the left. An engine's roar amplified the quick approach of a vehicle as it slithered down the street, moving side to side like a snake intent on attack. She watched in horror as the Jeep changed trajectory to head straight for her giggling aunt, who was still in the street. A hand pulled Coral back to safety. Aaron had let go of Ruby and stood, frozen, out of harm's way.

"Look out!" Coral screamed.

Mr. Penny shoved past her and grabbed Aunt Ruby just as the Jeep flew by, passing within inches of her. If he hadn't been there, Aunt Ruby would have been hurt or killed. Coral narrowed her eyes and shook her head at Aaron. He was a coward.

"Are you okay, Ruby?" Mr. Penny asked.

Aunt Ruby let out a loud breath, wide eyes fixed on the retreating Jeep. "I'm fine. Thank you."

49

Mr. Penny nodded as the Jeep skidded around a corner and was gone. "That was too close. Did anyone get the license plate?"

"Oh, no, dear. I didn't. Did you kids happen to notice the plates on that Jeep?" Mrs. Penny put her hand to her throat. Was she going to faint?

"No, Mom, I didn't," Beth said. "And Ben was too busy saving Coral to notice—right, Ben?"

He cleared his throat. "Yes, well, that Jeep was driving erratically. I didn't know if she was going to be hit or not. You and Mom were out of the way, and Dad saved Ruby."

Coral put her hand on Ben's arm and offered him a smile. "Thank you, Ben."

He looked away. "Welcome. No big deal."

A modest hero like his dad.

Mr. Penny looked them over to ensure they were okay. "Let's call it a night."

Aaron had his arm wrapped protectively around Aunt Ruby. "I'm *so* glad you're okay. My life flashed before my eyes when I thought that Jeep was going to hit you. I couldn't move. I was burdened down with fear, imagining life without you." He pulled her closer.

"Thank you."

Coral shook her head. He was imagining her dead before it happened, and she *thanked* him? Burdened down with fear, what did that even mean? He sure wasn't there when Ruby needed him, and he made sure *he* was okay. Coral scowled at the back of Aaron's peach shirt as she followed the group safely to the other side of the road. His shirt looked fairly expensive. A rich coward.

All conversations focused on the driver. They each had theories, but the only one that made sense was that he must have been drunk. Mr. Penny called and reported the incident, but there wasn't much that could be done with their limited information. The part that amazed Coral was how Aaron twisted the facts to look like the hero, while Mr. Penny didn't have much more to say about it after he made the call.

Coral was sick to her stomach and shaky, but she was comforted by Ben's presence behind her and Mr. Penny on full alert. His head was constantly in motion, scanning the street as they walked. Mrs. Penny and Beth talked quietly while Aaron clung to her aunt as if she'd run away from him.

Coral peered into the shadows, convinced they weren't alone.

***

From the darkness on the other side of the street, Kini watched it all happen. The driver was very good-looking, probably in his thirties, with long black hair and a chiseled face. He certainly didn't look drunk to her, and that swerve appeared intentional. She would have caught a shot of it too, if he had hit Ruby. She crouched down as they passed. She'd changed out of her muumuu into comfortable sweats and doubted they would recognize her, but better to be careful.

She'd study her pictures more closely later. Maybe this was why she'd been hired to follow this family. They headed back in the direction of the hotel. Mrs. Penny and her daughter were chattering away. The new boyfriend was all over Ruby now, but during the accident, he was useless. All looks and not much else to him. She knew the type.

Keeping a good distance, she followed them to the hotel. Her day was over if they went to bed. Then it would start all over the next day, bright and early, with a lengthy tour. She sighed. If she didn't need the money so badly—but she did. Next time she'd ask for more cash to tail people. It was time-consuming and quite often forced her to call in sick at the diner.

***

Ned parked the black Jeep, knowing he'd put enough distance between him and his target. A good test run and warning. It was obvious he couldn't attempt this again around Mr. Penny. That boyfriend, who wasn't even worth the time it would take to find out his identity, was useless. He didn't bother to call out to warn her. Now, that's a keeper. Not that it mattered anyway. She wouldn't be alive long enough to find out. She had until Maui to enjoy her life.

He'd noticed the lady in the shadows taking pictures and memorized her license plate. They might be working for the same people, but that didn't matter. She'd seen his face and most likely recorded it. That was a problem. He'd take care of her for free and save his boss some money. Bosses loved it when he did that for them.

He switched out the license plates. The owner would surely still be eating. The restaurant was one of those swanky types that took forever, the kind of place he never had time for. How confused would the owner be if the police showed up to question him on a hit-and-run? Ned laughed and started whistling.

51

***

Ruby ran her fingers through her hair and adjusted her flower. "Aaron and I are going to take a quick walk on the beach. I need to wind down after what just happened." Her eyes were huge with adoration.

"Yes, join us." Insincerity laced Aaron's tone.

"Can we go?" Beth asked.

"Not tonight, sweetheart. Your mother is tired. It's been a long, eventful day, especially after that crazy driver almost hit Ruby. I think we should turn in."

Mrs. Penny nodded. "Yes, that was scary. Plus, we have a big day ahead. That tour I booked is a twelve-hour day. We need to get to our meeting point in front of the hotel by six thirty, so we have to be up, dressed, and eating breakfast by six."

Beth pushed her braid back with a glance at Coral. "Can't we just rent a car and go see all the places ourselves?" Coral crossed her fingers but was certain Mrs. Penny had already bought the tickets because she was a planner.

Mr. Penny shook his head. "It would be too hard on your mom driving all day by herself. Ruby and I have to work, sweetheart. This way, someone else does the driving, and you all can enjoy yourselves."

"Okay, Dad," Ben quickly agreed.

Aunt Ruby was entangled with Aaron again, breaking away long enough to tell Coral to go ahead up to their room.

"I'll be up later. Good—" Once again, Aaron interrupted.

"Good night, and it was a pleasure meeting all of you." He quickly guided Aunt Ruby out the door.

When they got to their rooms, Mrs. Penny invited Coral in to watch a movie.

"Thanks, but I think I'll go to sleep."

"Make sure you ask for a wake-up call."

"I'll set my cell phone alarm."

"That works, but remember to charge it. I'll order room service for breakfast, so come over as soon as you're ready, and remember we have to leave here by six ten," Mrs. Penny concluded as Mr. Penny held the door open for his family.

"I'll be ready. Night."

"Dream good dreams," Mr. Penny added.

It wasn't that late, but Coral was tired and didn't bother to email Tara again. She skipped a shower and climbed into bed to listen to the ocean. After setting her alarm, the whooshing of the waves carried her to sleep without the expected replaying of the accident. Her dream quickly started again and was more vivid than ever before. Coral woke up just as she broke the water's surface. There had been a golden blur before she was jarred awake.

Reaching for her water bottle, her gaze met an unmade bed. It was almost midnight, and it wasn't like her aunt to stay out late—and with that snake! Coral yawned loudly and shook her head before sinking back into the soft bed. There were no more dreams. The alarm on her phone screamed the "good morning" song promptly at 5:30 a.m.

Rubbing her eyes and stretching, she took in her aunt's rumpled sheets. At least she'd come back at some point. She shuffled over to the notepad propped on the dresser, feeling like lead. *Have a great day. I will see you later. I'm meeting Aaron for breakfast.* Coral crumpled the message into a ball and threw it away. Scowling, she stomped to the bathroom.

D. L. Finn

Chapter 9
Seeing Oahu

As the steamy water flowed from the wide showerhead, Coral went through her daily routine, thinking about her aunt hanging all over a man who hadn't even attempted to save her life. She had to make Ruby see what a loser he was.

She arrived at the Pennys' suite by five forty-five. The food tray was loaded with eggs, waffles, a fruit platter, milk, and cereal. She plopped down next to Beth and nibbled on a waffle and some scrambled eggs. Everyone was groggy and quiet except Mrs. Penny, who was rushing about, coffee cup in hand.

"Oh dear, it's almost six! Did you all get something to eat?" She loaded a plate with a waffle, bacon, and some eggs. Ben scooped out the last bit of cereal from his paper bowl while Beth rebraided her hair.

"Yes, Mom, we all got breakfast," Beth replied for all of them.

"Well, it'll be a long day, and we won't eat again until lunchtime. I'm glad your dad got to eat before he left. Let's see, I have the tickets, sunscreen, water, some nuts, hats for all of us, and the camera. I should throw in some light wraps too."

Beth looked at Coral with a small smile at her mother's comment. Coral grinned back.

Mrs. Penny gulped down her food faster than Coral had ever seen her eat.

"Are you kids ready?" She grabbed the beach bag.

"Just a minute," Ben mumbled, running into the bathroom.

They reached the stop for the tour bus with fifteen minutes to spare. Coral gazed longingly at the ocean, where there were already a couple of surfers out. She wished they were spending the day at the hotel swimming and relaxing instead of cramming into a van with two other families.

An hour later, they made their first stop at Pearl Harbor. They hit the visitors center, where Mrs. Penny bought more souvenirs. There was a pathway lined with names—so many lives lost on December 7, 1941. Melancholy overwhelmed Coral as she read each name. Beth found her great-uncle's name and had Ben take her picture with it. Mrs. Penny was talking to the son of a survivor who was acting as a guide. She insisted on a picture with him, Beth, and Ben. Coral declined to be included. Soon they rode in a small boat across some choppy water to the memorial of the USS *Arizona*. She felt eerie standing over the watery grave of 1,100 men and seeing the oil that was still leaking from the ship.

The next stop on the tour was the Dole Plantation. They pulled up to what looked like a huge house with a long porch and *DOLE* spelled out in plants. They were guided through the world's longest maze on three acres and shown the eight hidden stations. A twenty-minute train ride through the plantation taught Coral all she needed to know about pineapples and James Dole. After they were treated to some pineapple chunks and juice, there was barely any time left to stroll through the huge tropical gardens.

Back in the van, Mrs. Penny perked up as they headed north. They passed a small town and took many pictures, in which Coral agreed to be included.

Finally they hit the breathtaking coastline. They veered off and made their way to the Polynesian Center just in time for a lunch of greasy pulled-pork sandwiches. Coral was hungry, which made the food taste better than it should have. After lunch they walked around to see all the huts and demonstrations. Beth hung close to Coral.

"Could you imagine living like this?" she asked.

"I could."

Coral threw a glance at Ben, who was withdrawn. His body language showed alertness, like a lion hunting its prey. She, on the other hand, was feeling more like an antelope instead of a lion after the night before.

They were guided through six villages and watched the locals prepare food and go about everyday life before the Spanish arrived. Coral continued to try to catch Ben's eye, with no luck. Dancers on a raft floating down the waterway captured her attention. She wished she was with them. It was easy to imagine living in a hut, making leis, lying on the beach in the warm sun, and cooking fish over an open fire. Basket making and hula dancing would have been enjoyable ways to pass the time.

Soon it was time for the hour-plus drive back to their drop-off point. There'd be stops on the way, including a waterfall. A feeling of being watched came over her as Ben remained aloof. Coral sighed.

After visiting the waterfall and taking pictures of some amazing views, she dozed off, confident that Beth and her mom would record every minute of their drive back to the hotel. She bolted awake only once and found Mrs. Penny napping too.

They caught the end of a colorful sunset right as they pulled up to the hotel. All she wanted to do was eat and go to bed. Tomorrow was going to be a big day. She would finally make her way to the island her parents had disappeared from.

They met up with Mr. Penny and her aunt to eat a quick dinner and head back to their rooms. Well, everyone but Aunt Ruby, who excused herself and left for the beach.

"Would you like to watch a movie with us?" Mrs. Penny's smile was tired.

"Not tonight. I need to pack, but thanks."

She swore a look of disappointment crossed Ben's face. As soon as she entered her room, she found an email from Tara.

I spent all day dancing. We put together a routine we'll perform at the end of class. My mom will tape it for you. Haley and I walked around with our parents and her brother. I'm positive you'd love New York. All the lights and people, it's so exciting. I got you something today that I know you'll love. I am going to dinner soon. Update me.

Coral started typing. She told Tara about everything that had been happening, including her aunt's new relationship and the photographer following them. She ended it with *Tomorrow we go to Maui. I hope to get some real answers there. You understand. I hope you are having fun and staying out of trouble. Miss you.*

She shut off the lights without packing. She rested on her bed, listening to the ocean's song as it caressed the shores until sleep washed over her like a billowy wave.

***

Kini sat out in front of the hotel. It had been tricky following the tour today, but she'd made it work by pretending to be with another tour at the stops.

She was proud of herself, playing the part in a short red wig, sunglasses, denim shorts, and an *I Love Hawaii* shirt. She pulled it off, though, and got some good pictures of them. Coral hadn't glanced her way once. That lovesick boy hadn't noticed her, even though he appeared to be scanning the crowds when his eyes weren't on the girl. The girl watched him when he wasn't looking. How cute. Puppy love.

Her job would have been so much easier if Ruby hadn't lingered on the beach with that man. Kini wanted to relax in front of the TV and unwind, but she had brought wine. She poured some into her coffee cup. Finally she'd be able to pay rent and the bills she was a month behind on. She hated it when that happened, and it seemed to happen often.

Again everyone went to their rooms, except Ruby. It was a repeat performance of the night before, kissing and laughing. At eleven Ruby finally headed back to her room. As the boyfriend left, Kini could have sworn he glanced her way and nodded.

She shook her head. *My mind's playing tricks on me.*

She gulped the rest of her wine and headed home. She had to be back tomorrow at seven to follow them to the airport. Then her job was finished, and she'd get paid. A smile appeared. Maybe she could get that new TV. She could put some of it on credit. And for once, she'd pick up a bottle of good wine. After all, she didn't have to pay every bill on time.

Chapter 10
A Guy with a Ponytail

Coral broke the surface of the water in the cave. Her eyes burned and watered, but she was able to make out a blurry gold city. Then a phone rang, and she sank back under the water.

She opened her eyes and found herself in bed.

"Thank you." Aunt Ruby mumbled and returned the phone to its cradle.

Coral sat up as her aunt burrowed under the covers. With a deep frown, she pulled herself from her dream sanctuary and headed to the bathroom. The floral suds washed away her sleepiness but not her frustrations. Not only had she not gotten a clear view of that golden city, her aunt had snuck in last night like a teenager. A creaky door and a narrow stream of light had woken Coral from a deep sleep. Her aunt had silently tiptoed across the room, then climbed into her bed. It wasn't that she didn't want her aunt to have a life, but did it have to be with that coward?

Sleep hadn't come easily after that. Her aunt's steady snore was background music as she replayed some of the strange events that had happened since they started their tropical vacation. There were a lot of questions with no answers.

Coral sighed heavily as she stepped out of the shower. The fluffy peach bath towel smelled of flowers, and she wrapped it tightly around her.

She swiftly dressed in jean shorts and a red-flowered T-shirt Mrs. Penny had bought her. Then she added black mascara, applied pink lipstick to her chapped lips, cleaned her glasses, and began to untangle her wet hair, which she gave up on and pulled into a ponytail. Her wilted lei hung on the hairdryer, its pleasing scent long gone. She tossed it in the trash, ready to move on to the next island.

After touching up the chip on her pedicure, she was ready.

Aunt Ruby hadn't moved.

"Aunt Ruby?"

"I'm awake." Aunt Ruby rubbed her eyes and stretched. "I guess I'd better get up."

"I'll get our suitcases ready."

"Would you? Thanks."

Packing went quickly, so she headed to the balcony to soak in the view one more time.

Finally Aunt Ruby emerged from the bathroom in the sundress she'd bought with Coral in Reno and a bright red lipstick that made her look even more tired. "We need to get going. We'll get some breakfast at the airport."

"I'm not hungry."

"You will be." Aunt Ruby grinned.

Coral shrugged as her aunt held on to that smile while zipping their overnight case shut. They all piled into the hotel van in what felt like zombie mode. Soon they were in line to board the plane. Coral was the last one, behind Ben.

She was nibbling on her pineapple breakfast bar when goosebumps popped up on her arms. Someone was watching. Holding her body still, she slowly moved her head and immediately found a man with his cell phone trained on them, taking pictures. Her heart raced as she fumbled through her bag for her cell phone.

"Ben, look to the right," Coral whispered urgently. "Someone is taking pictures of us again."

Ben was ready with his cell phone and got a shot, but not before the man started his retreat. He showed her the photo. "This guy has a long blond ponytail, see?"

"Yeah, doesn't look like the same guy that was in Reno—unless he has disguises, which would be even weirder." Coral turned to find Beth staring at her with a huge smile. She waved at them and then went back to her conversation with her mom.

Ben pointedly ignored his sister. "We have a guy with a ponytail and beard, blue hat, beige shorts, and a red shirt. Is average height, five ten or so, on the thin side, and appears to be in his thirties. You can tell that he's spent some time in the sun. Also, he's a bad dresser." He grinned.

It was great to see this humorous side of him. That would work well with Tara.

"If I remember correctly, the first guy was about the same size, but that's the only similarity I can remember. I wish I'd studied him more."

"This is a good start now that we have proof. I've been watching for someone since I saw the woman. On the tour I was on full alert after what happened to your aunt. I'm positive a woman's attention was focused on us. She kept moving, and I never got a clear shot of her. See?" Ben leaned in to show Coral three blurry pictures.

"Hard to tell, but she's the same size as the other lady, and I doubt that's a coincidence—but I didn't notice her, sorry."

"I was hoping to get another shot of our hotel lady so we could compare the two, but I didn't see her again."

"Well, we just have to keep watching."

"We will. And Coral, you aren't mad at me, are you?"

"Mad? Why would I be mad?"

"Well, I did kind of ignore you, but only to see who was following us."

"I might have wondered why." Coral returned her focus to her breakfast bar.

"I was going to explain when you came over to watch a movie, but you didn't."

"I was tired."

A huge smile lit up Ben's face. "Good. Let's keep alert and get some more pictures, in case we have to convince them." He nodded to his family and Aunt Ruby.

"Right." Coral smiled.

"Ticket." The man held his hand out. Ben handed it over, and Coral pulled hers out, ready. Before they entered the tunnel, they both glanced back, cameras in hand, to where the man had been, but he was gone.

***

Ned smiled to himself, fully aware that Coral had spotted him. He didn't care; his disguise was so complete she wouldn't realize he was the same person from Reno. Besides, no one would believe her, except maybe that lanky Harry Potter boy who even a blind man could see was crushing on her. Although he couldn't get rid of Coral Dover, there were no such restrictions for her aunt. His boss had updated him. They were positive that the girl would lead them to the very place they wanted her to.

Slipping into the restroom stall, he did a quick change into the ultimate tourist. A padded Hawaiian shirt, rimmed glasses, short brown hair, sandals, and a black fanny pack were the perfect disguise. He trashed the other items because he rarely used the same disguise twice.

Just to be safe, he took the next flight out to Maui, although he was positive of his ability to hide in plain sight. He'd managed to overhear where they'd be staying, so that wasn't a worry. Whistling a tune he made up, he approached the bar to order a nice cool, tropical drink. The name on his boarding pass was Bob Smith. He was an elementary school teacher from Texas with a perfect twang and knowledge of teaching sixth-graders. Everything was going so well, including his extra activities last night.

Chapter 11
Ocean View

Coral slept through the twenty-five-minute plane ride to Maui. After a dreamless nap, she opened her eyes just as the plane skidded hard to slow down on the Kahului Airport runway. She stretched and rubbed her eyes while Aunt Ruby closed her book. Mr. Penny was already removing their bag from the overhead compartment. When they exited the plane this time, no one greeted them. In the heavy tropical heat, they loaded their luggage into the back of a rented six-passenger SUV. Coral paused before stepping inside the vehicle, scanning the area for anyone taking pictures of them. There was nothing out of the ordinary. She pushed her way to the back row and sat next to Aunt Ruby.

The drive to their hotel at Kaanapali Beach was disappointing. Some of the areas looked similar to Nevada's barren, beige landscape. She shut her eyes and was soon asleep again.

Aunt Ruby nudged her. "Wake up, sleepyhead. We're here."

Coral grinned. This was how she'd imagined Maui—a palm-lined hotel on the ocean. It was hard not to burst out of the vehicle and dive headfirst into the inviting blue water.

Mr. Penny said, "I can drop you off at the hotel and park."

Mrs. Penny shook her head. "No, I need to walk. I'll stay with you."

"It'll be an uphill walk because the lot is pretty full."

"That's fine."

Beth twisted around and exploded into a narrative. "I wanted to tell you about this hotel, but you were sleeping. You're going to love it here. They have a torch-lighting ceremony every night at sunset. And there's an awesome swimming pool lined with waterfalls that wraps around a bar. You can order the food poolside too. They have the best chips and dip, and you go snorkeling around that cliff—some people scuba dive. I prefer scuba diving to snorkeling. Maybe you can learn and we can do that together someday. I've never been here when there wasn't a turtle at the beach. Oh, and there's a walkway connecting the hotels and a mall we can go to. So much to do here. This is my favorite island!"

Mrs. Penny smiled broadly at her daughter. "Yes, and you can try out that new underwater camera, Coral. I'd like to go to the aquarium today and maybe Christmas shop. Then tomorrow we can get an early start and do the Hana drive. You can come with us tomorrow, right, dear?"

Mr. Penny smiled and looked at Aunt Ruby in his rearview mirror. "I think we can wrap up work today, right, Ruby?"

Aunt Ruby glanced up from her phone. "Yes, oh, right. Sorry, I was texting Aaron. He cut off his vacation on Oahu early and is heading over to Maui on the next flight. Isn't that great?"

"Wonderful," Mrs. Penny replied.

Beth's face almost glowed. To her, Aunt Ruby and Aaron's connection was a love story coming to life.

Mrs. Penny turned around. "You have certainly hit it off with him, and he lives near us. I know he said he works with Dunning. What kind of company does he work for?"

Mr. Penny and Ben both turned their heads like they were trying to hear her response better. So far, Aaron had avoided that topic.

"He can't talk about it. Security and all." Aunt Ruby's brows furrowed deeply.

Mrs. Penny smiled. "Of course, I completely understand. Does he have any kids, or has he been married before?"

"No, like me, he's never been married. Always waiting for the right one. No kids either. We already talked about that. He's more into dogs than kids, which works for me." Aunt Ruby blushed. "Of course, we're both happy you're here, Coral. I mean, he's excited to get to know you. What I meant to say was we don't want to have our own kids."

Coral nodded and looked away. It wasn't her choice to live with her aunt. Whatever. Soon she'd be out on her own, and Aunt Ruby could return to her peaceful life.

Mr. Penny broke the awkward silence as he pulled into a parking space. "Of course you love having Coral around. Who wouldn't? It's nice you and Aaron are on the same life page. Let's get our luggage and check in."

He helped his wife out of the car. Coral hoped she'd meet someone who looked at her the way Mr. Penny looked at his wife. And she was positive she wanted kids someday. No man would change her mind on that one.

"Yes, it's all happening so fast, but I feel like he may be the one," Aunt Ruby gushed, stepping out ahead of Coral.

"Take your time and get to know him first, dear," Mrs. Penny advised.

Mr. Penny and Ben had already managed to handle all their luggage.

"Yes, we plan to continue dating once we're back home." Aunt Ruby's attention was pulled to her phone.

"Good. It's important to be friends too." Mrs. Penny looked up at her husband with a smile as he affectionately kissed the top of her head.

"Right." Aunt Ruby didn't look up from her furious texting.

"I can carry my luggage," Coral offered.

"We have it." Mr. Penny's paced quickened.

Beth took over the conversation again as they walked through the hot parking lot. "You are going to love the Hana drive, Coral. The only bad part is the road is super narrow, and it makes Mom nervous driving on it. But there are *so* many places to stop and waterfalls everywhere. There's a black beach at the end where we always swim, and a red beach too."

"I can't wait." Coral watched Ben and his dad haul their bags up the steep hill. He flashed a smile at her and nodded as he adjusted his awkward load at the hotel entrance.

She nodded back and held up her cell phone, making a quick sweep of the parking lot. No one was taking pictures this time. They soon hit the top of the hill and were entering the hotel. The cool air was a welcome change. After making sure no one had a camera pointed at them, she took in the cheerful lobby. Red ornaments and tinsel covered the indoor shrubbery. The lighting was green and red, and one side of the lobby opened to the azure sea. A gentle, salty breeze wafted into the room.

"We're all set," Mr. Penny announced.

Coral pointed. "I want to get a picture of everyone. Stand there with the ocean as a background." She aimed her cell phone at the group as everyone pushed together without argument.

"Okay, now smile." Aunt Ruby wore the biggest smile. Coral captured three good pictures of her and the Pennys.

Beth held her phone up. "I want a picture too, Coral. You get in this one. Take my spot by my brother. Closer, everyone. Ready? Cheese!"

Coral was squished up against Ben.

"Perfect, but one more. This time, I want everyone in it. Closer, everyone." Beth pushed in and held the camera. Her arms weren't long enough, so Ben grabbed it and got everyone in the shot.

Coral took a quick shot of the white dolphin water fountain draped with red lights and flowers in the center of the lobby. Unlike the hotel on Oahu, there wasn't a Christmas tree. Maybe they could get a small one to decorate their room.

"They upgraded us. I think you guys are going to like your rooms."

Ben and his dad loaded their luggage onto the baggage cart, so Coral took in the views. They were perched above all the activities outside the hotel. There was a beautiful green lawn and the pool Beth had mentioned, but beyond all that were the beach and the ocean—moana or kai, as the list of Hawaiian terms on the wall called it. She could understand something so beautiful having two names. Off to the right, a cliff jutted out, ending the beach, but in the other direction, it looked like the beach continued as far as her eyes could see. There were people everywhere, including on the cement walkway above the beach Beth had told her about. Coral couldn't wait to explore. This time she had over a week and a half to enjoy herself and planned to spend most of it in the moana.

"Ready? Follow me." Mr. Penny led the way to the elevator.

"It's a long maze to the rooms if we're staying in the same wing we did last time. It's so worth it, though," Beth explained breathlessly.

She was right. By the time they reached their rooms, it seemed as if they'd walked forever. They had three adjoining suites with stunning views of the ocean, a small island, and cliffs below them. There was a room for Mr. and Mrs. Penny, one for Beth and Ben, and one for Aunt Ruby and Coral.

Aunt Ruby put her suitcase on the stand. "Isn't this wonderful?"

"It's everything I imagined it would be. I can't wait to snorkel."

"This is a great place to snorkel, but there's another spot I want to take you to at some point. You'll find the turtles are friendly, but don't touch them. It's against the law and carries a big fine. I'm glad Mrs. Penny is taking you to the aquarium today. You'll learn about the local sharks. The Hawaiians have great respect for them, and so should we. Well, I should go meet up with Mr. Penny. Aaron will be landing on the island in a couple of hours. He got a room right next to us. Lucky, right?" Aunt Ruby's happiness illuminated the room.

"Very lucky." Coral felt like bugs were crawling all over her. She couldn't shake the feeling something bad was about to happen, and it had nothing to do with the local sharks.

"See you later. We'll be taking a taxi, so you guys can have the car. Be good, and listen to Mrs. Penny. She should be calling you soon. Bye!"

Coral immediately unpacked and then sat on the balcony, which had a small white table, two chairs, and a lounge. Below their room was a grassy area surrounded by a low metal fence. Off to the left was a lone torch and a black rock cliff that people were climbing up to jump into the ocean. Coral hoped exploring that other island was on their itinerary. The conversation from the people snorkeling below floated up to her. She was unable to see them, but it was like she was down there with them. She couldn't wait to be one of them, exploring the ocean.

Grabbing an apple from the complimentary basket of fruit, she settled into the lounge chair, donned her sunglasses, and took a deep breath of tropical perfection.

"Stingray!" someone yelled below.

Springing up, she peered down, hoping the stingray would breach the water in a visible spot. She wished for binoculars. At least whales would be easier to see. It was the season for the humpback whale migration, and she was determined to see one.

***

When Ned's plane landed at the airport, his camera was ready. He'd managed to get some good shots of Ruby Hyde's boyfriend, Aaron Harvey. He was well dressed and carried himself like he was important. Ned wondered if he could take him down with Ruby but thought that might need approval. Changing his phone setting from airplane mode, he inquired and received an immediate response.

Your request is denied. Do not involve or injure him. It would attract too much attention, and you'll be heavily fined. Nor will you be paid extra for taking out the other operative, but you'll not be fined either. She was expendable. Right now, your only target is Ruby Hyde, no one else.

Continue to get as many photographs as you can. Awaiting your report. Do not disappoint us.

Ned sighed. That was a shame, because he'd have enjoyed taking down that coward. He snapped another picture of Aaron, who was furiously texting a message, probably to Ruby. Soon she wouldn't be replying. He knew where Aaron Harvey was headed when he overheard him calling the hotel—the same place as the rest, of course.

Hawaiian music played in the background as he waited for his luggage. Flipping through his camera, he was glad he'd taken pictures of the other operative. It was unlucky for her that he wasn't in disguise when she saw him driving the Jeep. He'd delete the images of Karen—who went by Kini—later. Holding on to things that could implicate you was never a smart thing to do, especially when a murder was involved.

In the first picture he'd taken, she was sleeping soundly. In the second picture, she looked confused when he introduced himself and was not happy to meet him. The third picture captured her fear when she realized why he was there. That was his favorite.

She was no longer a threat. He was doing her a favor. Kini was alone and poor, and they weren't paying her what they paid him. She didn't have anything to look forward to. No family—her neighbor had been eager to chat. So enthusiastic, she'd even offered him a slice of cake fresh from the oven. He'd declined, though, saying he was surprising his "cousin" Kini with dinner. His disguise had been perfect. Tan makeup, long black hair, a beard, and padded clothes. No one would ever be able to find him by that description.

Ned picked up his black suitcase, filled with all his disguises, and waited for Aaron to retrieve his. Following close behind him, he ended up at the same car rental counter. As they walked away to their separate cars, he smiled at what was ahead.

Chapter 12
Maui Tourists

The ringing phone interrupted Coral's peace. It was a reminder to meet Mrs. Penny, Beth, and Ben at the pool for lunch. They were deep into burgers and chips by the time she reached them. Beth handed her a plate with a huge cheeseburger. The locally made chips were incredible, with just the right amount of salt, garlic, and oil. She wished she could have gone for a swim first, but she still enjoyed their early lunch.

Before she knew it, they were on their way to the aquarium. After they parked, a loud horn sounded. "What is that?" Coral yelled, wondering if she should run. No one else seemed concerned.

"They're testing their system in case of an emergency, like a tsunami. Scared me the first time I heard it. I think they do it once a month. If it were real, you'd know it," Mrs. Penny said.

"Well, it's loud," Beth protested.

"It is. You kids run ahead, and I'll lock the car up."

Just as they started walking, Coral realized she had forgotten her sunglasses.

"I'll be right back," she said to Beth. Ben was already waiting at the door, staring at his phone. She rushed back to the car. As she got closer, she saw Mrs. Penny throwing back another handful of pills. She froze.

Again? What was wrong with her?

The siren stopped, and Coral hustled away without her sunglasses.

"I thought you went to get your sunglasses." Beth stared at Coral's empty hands and face.

"I think I left them back at the hotel."

"Oh, well, we'll be indoors most of the time."

Ben held her sunglasses out.

"They were next to mine. I didn't know that's why you went back to the car, sorry. You know, with the sirens going." He looked away.

"Oh, thank you."

When their hands touched, she felt a bolt of electricity shoot through her. He pulled away like he'd been burned.

"You're welcome," he mumbled, red-faced, before returning to his phone.

Maybe it was just a simple electric shock. It was hard to believe that she'd been around Ben her whole life and ignored him until now. He was always just Beth's brother. Tara's crush had opened Coral's eyes. Finding out he was a guitarist in a band made her realize there was much more to him than what she had initially thought. All the superficial stuff that impressed Tara didn't matter to Coral. For her, the fact he was a good person was the most important thing. He'd not only saved her life but was patient with his sister and helped his mom. He was also helping her figure out why people were taking pictures of them. Tara had picked a great guy to like.

They were photographed out front by the Maui Ocean Center fountain, this time by aquarium staff and not a random stranger. Coral predicted Mrs. Penny would buy the picture. While Mrs. Penny was busy taking pictures inside, Coral scanned the area. No one was watching them. A hammerhead shark swam over her head, making her jump. The tubular walkway passed through a huge tank filled with every imaginable sea creature. A tiger shark, very common in Hawaii, swam above them. She read a sign about swimming in the sea when they exited the tunnel. *Don't act like a seal* seemed like good advice, and *Stay out of cloudy waters where the sharks can't tell their prey from humans* was even better.

Coral wasn't worried, though. The chances of a shark attacking her weren't very high. They continued walking and looking at tanks of fish. Jellies had always fascinated her. Outside they touched sea stars and enjoyed the sea turtle tank, and then Mrs. Penny announced it was time to go.

She hurried them to the car without buying the picture taken of them out front. Although that was very unlike her, she did want to shop, and that was her norm. They drove to a little town called Lahaina. Their first stop was the Hard Rock Café, which housed an Elvis Presley collection. Mrs. Penny was a huge Elvis fan and had Beth take her picture by all the displays.

"I do this every time, right, kids?"

"You do, Mom!"

As they moved along through the town, a huge banyan tree with the biggest trunk she had ever seen captured her attention.

"This tree was a gift from India in the 1800s. It's also one of the biggest ones in America," Mrs. Penny stopped to explain.

Coral marveled at its size but couldn't get a picture of the whole thing where they were. The branches went out in many directions, and the trunk looked as if a bunch of branches had formed together to make it. She loved all the dangling limbs. It was an amazing sight.

Finally they were inside the air-conditioned Lahaina Cannery Mall, where Mrs. Penny guided them from store to store. Ben caught Coral's eye and shrugged, signaling with his cell phone that he was on alert. She held up her phone in reply.

She purchased a couple of postcards but nothing else. The one pair of binoculars she saw were over $100, so she didn't get them. Nor did she pick up a swim mask since they were going to rent snorkel sets. Once again, Mrs. Penny found T-shirts for all of them, towels, and a dress for herself with a matching shirt for Mr. Penny. She got Aunt Ruby another dress—this time in ruby red—and a matching one in coral for Coral, which she insisted, again, would be for Christmas.

When someone started playing "Stairway to Heaven" on a ukulele, Coral was shocked to find that it was Ben. He was so completely engrossed in what he was doing that he didn't notice her watching him. He was good.

After they'd covered most of the mall, Ben was loaded down with his mother's purchases. They made their way back to the blue SUV and then to the hotel. No new email from Tara. After they deposited their new treasures in their rooms, it was time to meet Mr. Penny and Aunt Ruby at the luau.

"Over here!" Aunt Ruby waved from a long wooden table.

"We had a wonderful day," Mrs. Penny said to Mr. Penny as he got up to pull her chair out and kiss her cheek.

"Get anything good today?" Aunt Ruby asked Coral, as Ben and Beth seated themselves across from them.

"Some postcards and stuff. The aquarium was cool, and we got to walk through a tube with sharks swimming above us."

"Good! I wish I could have gone, but tomorrow will be fun, right?" Aunt Ruby checked her phone.

"I can't wait. Beth has told me so much about it." Coral glanced over at Beth, who was smiling.

"It's an amazing drive. Maybe we'll see some whales too. I overheard someone say they saw one here yesterday. We can go out on a boat tour—" Aunt Ruby was interrupted by applause welcoming a group of hula dancers to the stage.

The show had begun, and they turned their attention to the stage. Coral took pictures of the first group of young dancers. They were so graceful, and she knew that each motion told part of a story.

I could watch this all night.

In between dances, when no one was paying attention to her, she turned her camera to get a picture of Ben. She smiled and sent it to Tara along with one of the family from earlier. Maybe now she would finally respond. She did a quick check to make sure no one was taking their picture. Everyone was focused on the show, including Ben. His hair was unruly, like it always was, and his eyes were wide and expressive. His glasses made his tanned face look stronger, and his black T-shirt showed off his broad, well-defined shoulders. Coral wondered why she used to think his glasses weighed down his face. They did the complete opposite.

A new group of dancers came out, pulling her attention back. They reminded her of ocean waves. The muumuu-wearing hostess explained what the barefoot dancers in grass skirts and flowers were doing. How their arms told stories and how long each of them had been dancing. Coral listened like there was going to be a test at the end. After another dance the women left, and the stage filled with a group of good-looking men. The drums pushed the fast music, and the men kept up with it while grabbing torches and lighting them. The performances enthralled the crowd. Coral didn't want it to end, but it soon did, making way for dinner.

In a formal ceremony, they dug up the specially prepared whole pig from the pit where it had been cooking for hours. It was carried to a table and carved for the feast. People lined up to get food while others visited booths to buy local produce and wooden carvings. Mrs. Penny wanted them to eat first before they shopped. Besides the pork, beans, green salad, chicken, fish, and fruit, there were limited options. A few people had a gray paste on their plate, yet no one was eating it. Coral learned it was poi.

"We've all tried it, Coral. You should too," Mrs. Penny encouraged.

"Okay." Coral scooped some on her plate. It looked horrible.

"You won't like it," Ben warned.

Beth frowned at her brother. "It's made from the taro root and is important in the Hawaiian diet. Plus, it's sacred to them," she shared, adding some to her plate. "Most people don't like it, but it's not bad. You eat it with your fingers."

After they sat down, Coral tried the poi and immediately spat it out. It was awful. Ben laughed heartily, and Beth looked pained.

"Oh, I thought you'd like it. I think it's tropical. It's just cooked taro that they mash up and add water to. Sorry," Beth said.

Ben was still smiling as he began eating.

"No problem. Just not my thing, I guess." Coral guzzled her pineapple juice to kill the aftertaste.

There was no comparison to their earlier meal of delicious burgers. They turned away from the bland food to watch the sunset and torch-lighting ceremony in silence while Mrs. Penny wandered off to see what wares they were selling. The red, yellow, and orange blended in a ball of fury right as a man dove into the ocean from the cliff. Then the colorful show disappeared behind the sea. The scene left Coral relaxed and happy.

"Isn't this bowl great?" Mrs. Penny asked, rejoining the group at the end of the sunset.

"It is." Aunt Ruby touched the large, wood-grained bowl.

"I think we should walk off all that food." Mrs. Penny eyed her husband for a reaction.

"That's a great idea. And that bowl will look nice on our dinner table." He relieved her of the weight of it.

"It will, won't it?" Mrs. Penny beamed.

"Aaron said he's waiting for us." Aunt Ruby looked around for him.

He was smart to avoid the poi.

Right on cue, Aaron showed up. "How was the luau? I'm sorry I missed it. I had some business to attend to." He kissed her aunt's cheek gently.

"The show was great, like most I've been to. The food was okay," Mr. Penny replied.

"I thought it was wonderful, but it would have been perfect if you had been there." Ruby beamed at Aaron.

73

"Well, my day is perfect now that I've seen you." He grabbed her hand and pulled her into a hug.

Beth watched them like she was watching a movie. Coral hoped she wasn't going to cry if they got too sappy. They started down the cement walk, the beach and ocean on one side and hotels, restaurants, and stores on the other. Coral kept up her surveillance and made sure no one was pointing a camera at them. Beth and her mom were pointing to a mall.

Oh, no.

She tried to think of a way to stop the oncoming shopping spree when some people come out of the ocean with their snorkels.

"That's what we need." Aaron pointed to the snorkeling gear.

Coral nodded. "Yes, I can't wait to snorkel. We should rent some at the hotel before we go to Hana tomorrow."

Ruby glanced at Aaron with a blushing smile. "That's a good idea. I'll rent them now. I remember seeing a store on the way in from the airport. Let me check when it closes."

Mrs. Penny shook her head. "The hotel rentals will be fine, Ruby. Don't worry about it. I doubt we will have time to snorkel on the Hana drive."

"I know the place you're talking about, and it has much better quality," Aaron said, ignoring Mrs. Penny's comment. "I'd go there to rent them."

"You think so, Aaron? Okay. Well, they close in an hour. I'll head over now. Would you like to come with me?" Aunt Ruby grinned.

"I'd love to, but I have one more errand to run. I'll meet you back here. Then we can head over to that club we saw. You be careful, Ruby. I don't want anything to ever happen to you."

"I'm always careful."

"See you soon. Meet you in the lobby in an hour and a half? I bid the rest of you good night, and I'll see you in the morning. I won't keep your aunt out too late, Coral. Don't worry." Aaron winked and kissed Aunt Ruby's forehead before he walked away. Coral was surprised he didn't ask Aunt Ruby to walk back with him.

"I'll see you in a bit," Aunt Ruby called after him. He held up a hand in a wave without looking back.

"Good night, Aaron," Mrs. Penny called. "It's been another long day. Do you mind not shopping tonight, Coral?"

"Oh, no. I don't mind," Coral said quickly, trying not to smile.

"Okay, good. I know you have some Christmas shopping left to do, and so do we. Don't worry, we'll have plenty of time to do it."

Coral found Ben searching the crowd. He shook his head, signaling that no one was snapping photos of them.

"I won't be out late. You can hang out with the Pennys tonight, right?"

"Of course she can. I'm sure the kids will be watching movies." Mrs. Penny looked at Ben and Beth.

"That's the plan." Beth's face lit up, making her eyes sparkle like sapphires.

"Okay. Unless you want me to go with you, Aunt Ruby."

"No need. I'm meeting Aaron at the club and won't be coming back here first. I'll see you in the morning. Don't wait up for me. Good night, everyone."

"Drive carefully," Mr. Penny warned.

"I will." Aunt Ruby was already engrossed in her cell phone as she hurried off.

D. L. Finn

Chapter 13
Movie Time

Coral's stomach felt heavy. She couldn't shake the bad feeling she had watching her aunt leave. Aside from strangers snapping their photos and Aunt Ruby almost being run over, everything had been fine since they got to Maui. *Time to chill.*

The elevator thumped to a stop.

"Come to our room. We can decide on a movie," Beth said.

"Let me change first."

"Do I get any say in the movie?" Ben startled Coral.

"Of course! We won't force you to sit through a love story or dance movie—unless you want to," Beth teased.

"Maybe we can all agree on *Indiana Jones and the Kingdom of the Crystal Skull* since it was filmed in Hawaii? You can watch the Elvis movie with Mom later."

"Do you mind watching that movie, Coral? I don't hate *Indiana Jones*," Beth said.

"I don't mind. It's a good movie."

"Okay, see you in a few." Beth ran in the door behind her brother.

Coral almost slipped into her PJs but thought that might be weird for Ben. It was strange that she was worried about that for the very first time. She stood out on the balcony and listened to the ocean, breathing in the salt air. She was filled with a happiness that had been missing since her parents had disappeared. So why was that foreboding there?

Maybe because bad things have happened to me in the past.

Maybe it was time to let them go and move on with her life—or maybe not. She wasn't sure, but this was the place she'd figure it out. Coral sighed and sank into the chair with her cell phone. She smiled when she opened her phone to a welcome distraction: an email from Tara.

Coral! So, sorry, I haven't responded to you. I've been SO busy. Thanks for sending me the pictures. Everyone looks like they are having a great time. Next time I want a picture of you. The second picture of Ben is super cute. He looks good with a tan.

I'm glad you and your aunt are OK. How scary she almost got hit!

The classes are awesome. You'd like them, especially the modern class. It's a brutal schedule, though, but Haley is in all my classes. Her family is staying in New York the whole time too. They took my family and me out to dinner last night. I told you they are from Lake Tahoe, right? Only an hour away. And Haley's brother, Sam, well, we kind of hit it off. I have found my next boyfriend—seriously, I think he is the one.

He's a senior and has a blue 4x4 pickup for when it snows so that we can see each other every weekend. He has the bluest eyes and the prettiest wavy blond hair and snowboards, plays in a band, and loves to go to parties. We are so much alike—Haley's twin. I'll send you a picture of us later. You'll like them both, I promise. They remind me of us. Sam super outgoing and Haley more introverted . . . and I like them both.

So, become friends with Ben. Maybe you two can get together. I can see that, can't you? Then we could double date. Drag the introverts out. Ha! Glad you are getting to know each other. I told you he wasn't creepy, just quiet—like you. Keep me posted. And have fun. I'll try to write back soon. Right now, I gotta go. Love you, Tara

Coral sighed. Tara never wasted time when it came to guys. Her complete opposite. It was a relief she didn't have to try to set up Ben and Tara. *How weird is it to like Beth's brother?* She stopped in her tracks. She did like him, didn't she? Laughing and slipping into sweats, she grabbed her pillow and headed next door. She settled in next to Beth, glancing over at Ben. The room smelled like aftershave. Ben looked directly at her and smiled.

This should be interesting.

"Ready? We have sodas in the fridge and some microwave popcorn," Beth announced.

"I'm okay. Maybe later."

"Ben?" Beth asked.

"Later for me too. Like Coral said." He looked at her again.

A pleasant shiver went through her body as she greeted his stare with a smile. Ben grabbed the remote and switched on *Indiana Jones.* They hadn't gotten too far into the movie when Coral's phone rang.

She didn't recognize the number. "Hello?"

"We're calling this number from a patient's cell phone. Are you related to Ruby Hyde?"

Coral went pale and started shaking. "Yes, she's my aunt. Why?" Her voice trembled.

Ben turned off the movie. The caller identified themselves as a nurse from Maui Memorial. "I'm sorry to inform you there was an accident. Your aunt is with the doctor now."

Coral couldn't catch her breath. "An accident? Is she okay?"

There was a pause and a sound of papers being shuffled before the nurse spoke again. "I can't give out any more information over the phone. You need to come in, and if you're a minor, you'll need to have an adult with you." Coral numbly wrote down the address.

"Who was that? What happened?" Beth's eyes were huge.

"Aunt Ruby was in a car accident, but they wouldn't tell me anything else. The hospital got my number from her cell phone. I need to get to her."

Ben raced out of the room as Beth sank down next to Coral.

"I'm so sorry."

Coral's phone rang again, making them both jump.

"Hello?"

"Coral. This is Aaron. I just got a call from the hospital—your aunt was in an accident. I'm on my way there. You stay where you are, and I'll call you with details when I know more."

"No, I need to be there, Aaron. The Pennys will take me to the hospital. I'll see you there." Coral tossed the phone on the bed and stood up.

Ben burst into the room, pushing his hair back. "I told Dad. He's calling for a ride to take us to the hospital. Mom's tired, so you need to stay here with her, Beth."

"No, I should go," Beth protested. She was already up and standing next to Coral.

"What if Mom needs something? You know how much she depends on you. I'll keep you updated." Ben firmly shook his head at his sister.

D. L. Finn

Beth didn't argue.

They waited by the hotel's front entrance until a white Toyota pulled up. The driver, older, with straggly gray hair, assured them it would take only thirty-five minutes to get to the hospital. Coral had never been so scared and worried in her life, except when she'd heard her parents had been in an accident. It was happening all over again, but this time at least she knew where her aunt was—just not how she was.

Mr. Penny sat silently next to Coral with his arm around her in the back seat. Ben was on the other side. The drive to the hospital felt like an eternity. Ben seemed intent on memorizing the dark scenery they were passing. This was one time when Mrs. Penny's or Beth's talk might have helped. Coral was left alone with her racing thoughts. Her aunt had almost been run over on Oahu. This had to be more than a coincidence. The only new thing in their lives since this started was Aaron.

***

Ned knew they wouldn't spot him entering the hospital wearing a nurse's uniform as his disguise. He'd already ditched the protective gear he had worn when he crashed into Ruby's blue SUV. Although he knew there'd be no traces of him inside, he still set the truck he'd stolen on fire to be safe. The insurance inspectors would most likely believe the fire was due to impact. He smiled at the confusion the authorities would face trying to figure out where the driver had gone.

One thing that hadn't worked out the way he'd planned was that Ruby Hyde was still alive. He had been so sure she was dead. How anyone could have survived that direct hit in the driver's door was a mystery, but she had. He shook his head, knowing she should have been the priority. It had been a mistake focusing on the truck and not dealing with her. He didn't usually make mistakes.

A car had pulled up just as the truck he'd stolen burst into flames, and he had to hide in the tropical foliage. As he'd planned, it was an easy place to disappear quickly. The older woman, her cell phone in hand, had run straight to the burning truck. She looked around, then peered into the darkness, using her phone for light.

"Anyone there?" the woman had called. "Hello?"

She walked to almost the exact spot where Ned was hiding. Just a few more steps, and she would have ended up another victim.

"If anyone is out there, help is on the way," the woman had said, shining her light around the area. Ned remained still as she moved on to Ruby.

The good Samaritan checked Ruby's pulse and then tried talking to her, with no luck. No response was good. Camouflaged, Ned watched until the ambulance and fire truck arrived at the same time. The paramedics carefully loaded Ruby onto a gurney. The firefighters had to jump back when the flaming truck exploded. A police car screeched to a stop with lights and sirens screaming. That was Ned's cue to go.

He jogged along the side of the road, staying in the brush for over a mile. The only vehicles he'd seen were the ambulance—lit up like a Christmas tree—taking Ruby to the hospital and a tow truck. Finally he reached his rental and sped toward the hospital. Parking near the ER, he watched the ambulance leave. He kept on his brown wig and glasses because they were one of his best disguises. He entered the busy ER and quickly blended in with the staff.

He heard all he needed to know. Ruby Hyde had extensive brain damage and wasn't expected to make it through the night. *Perfect.* He shot off a text to his boss: *She isn't dead yet. Extensive brain damage. She is not expected to make it through the night and out of the way.*

Before he could put his phone away, a quick response sent a vibration through his palm. *Unfortunate. Keep a close eye on Coral. This shock should bring about change. Take more pictures. Update when you know more.*

Ned had never had a job go as badly as this one, especially after planning so, so carefully. He stayed in character as Ron, the cheerful nurse with a proper ID hanging around his neck. He whistled as he walked down the narrow corridors, waving to everyone he met. No one questioned his presence.

D. L. Finn

Chapter 14
A Time to Heal

Mr. Penny, Ben, and Coral rushed past Ron, the nurse, in search of information. They were referred to a young doctor sitting at the nurses' station.

"I'm Dr. Lee. You're her family?" the doctor asked, holding a clipboard. He looked more like a surfer than a knowledgeable man of medicine.

"Yes we are. I'm Robert Penny, and this is my son, Ben. Coral Dover is Ruby's niece," Mr. Penny replied, adding, "Ruby is Coral's guardian."

Coral couldn't speak. Her throat felt like it was closing up on her, and tears were threatening to flood her face.

Dr. Lee looked at Coral and smiled weakly. "We have Ms. Hyde stabilized right now, which is good. I know you were told she was in a car accident."

Mr. Penny nodded grimly. "What happened?"

Dr. Lee stared at the clipboard. "The only information I have is someone drove by right after the accident happened and called 911. From what I understand, the driver from the other car is missing. When the paramedics arrived, they found Ms. Hyde had a strong pulse, but she was unconscious. She's still in this condition. Do you know of any allergies or medical conditions she might have?"

"No. Nothing I know of. Coral?" Mr. Penny asked.

"Nothing besides she wears glasses. Is she going to be okay, Doctor?" Coral met the doctor's gaze in a silent plea for him to answer in the affirmative.

Dr. Lee couldn't hide his sympathy for Coral. He blinked hard. "Well, she has a badly sprained shoulder and a broken foot. There are lots of contusions, which will heal. It's her head we're concerned with because of the coma. There's no way of knowing how much brain damage she's sustained right now. Tonight will be critical. All we can do is monitor her and wait."

"Thank you. So if she makes it through the night . . . " Coral couldn't finish the rest of her question.

Dr. Lee glanced at Mr. Penny, who nodded. "We'll remain hopeful that this is a temporary condition."

Coral nodded. "I know she'll be okay."

Dr. Lee tugged at his white coat. "Yes, it's important to keep a positive attitude. This is a standard question, so don't let it worry you, but did Ms. Hyde have a medical directive in place in case something happened to her? Did she sign a donor card?"

"A what?" Coral's voice sounded distant, like an echo.

Mr. Penny grimaced. "She's never spoken of either, but we don't need to worry about that right now, do we, Doctor?"

Dr. Lee's face reddened. "No. Not yet. I'll keep you updated. Will you be waiting here?"

Coral put her hands on her hips and threw out her chest. "I'm not leaving."

Dr. Lee offered her another weak smile. "Okay. Then you'll be updated as soon as we know anything."

Mr. Penny jotted his number on a piece of paper from the ER desk. "Let me give you my cell phone number."

"Thank you. I'll add that to the chart. The chapel is down that way, and the cafeteria has vending machines with hot drinks. The nurse will come to get you when you can see her." Dr. Lee scurried away.

"Thank you," Mr. Penny called out. There was no response.

"I'm going to call Mrs. Penny and let her know what's going on. I'll be right back." He rushed out through the glass doors.

"Okay." Coral's voice was almost a whisper, and she wasn't sure he heard her.

"I'm sorry." Ben pushed his glasses back.

Coral sank into a chair. "Thanks. I'm glad you're here."

"I'll do what I can to help you through this. Just tell me what you need." In an awkward move, he sat next to her and put a hand on her shoulder. It sent a shiver down her arm. "You cold? I can ask for a blanket. Hospitals are always cold."

"No. I think it's just all the emotions running through me. There's nothing I need now except not to be alone. Thanks." If she weren't so numb, she'd be crying, like when she'd heard about her parents. It was scary how emotionless she felt—like a robot.

"No problem." He smiled shyly.

Mr. Penny returned just as Aaron came out of the ER hall.

"Oh, you guys came. I told Coral to wait until I had more information. Have you spoken to anyone yet?"

"Yes, the doctor spoke with us just a few moments ago. You were back with her?"

"Yes, he just updated me, and I finally got to see her. Coral shouldn't see her like this, don't you agree?" Aaron raised an eyebrow to Mr. Penny. He reminded her of a villain from a Disney movie, but she couldn't place which one.

"I think we should ask her what she wants to do. Don't you?" Coral had never heard Mr. Penny use such a firm tone.

"Well, she's a child, and I thought adults should be making the calls, but if you think that's best . . . "

"First, take me to Ruby. I want to see her for myself. Kids, I'll be right back. Coral, you decide if you want to see her or not, okay?"

Coral nodded, and they left. "He's creepy," she whispered to Ben.

"He is."

"I keep wondering if it's just coincidence that my aunt was almost run down on Oahu and now a car accident?" Coral finally said it out loud.

"I've been thinking the same thing."

"You have? So I'm not crazy."

"No, you're not."

"Thanks. It's just I've spent the last eight years wanting to come to the place where my parents went missing, to see—" Coral clamped her mouth shut.

Ben nodded. "To see how your dream ends?"

Coral rose from her seat. "What? How did you know?"

Ben looked down at the floor. "I overheard you talking to my dad. I should have walked away, but you would have seen me, so I stayed where I was."

"You were spying on us?"

"I? What? No. I didn't know what to do, honestly."

"No wonder you've always avoided me."

Ben shook his head. His eyes reminded her of a scared puppy. "I wasn't avoiding you. I just never knew how to approach someone like you. Okay, that didn't come out right. I meant you're smart and beautiful and way out of my league, and—I'm so sorry, Coral. This isn't the time for dumb statements like that."

Coral felt her jaw drop. She reached out and laid her hand on his arm. "That wasn't dumb, but you're right, not the time for it. So you know I'm—" She pulled back from Ben when Mr. Penny walked into the waiting room and folded her arms tightly, squeezing her ribs. "How is she?"

"She's pretty banged up but breathing on her own. Do you want to see her? You could sit by her side. I feel like she'd know you're there with her, although Aaron told them he's her fiancé, so we must deal with that," Mr. Penny replied, wrapping his arm around Coral's tensed shoulders.

She glanced over at Ben and then met Mr. Penny's gaze. "I don't care what Aaron claims. She's *my* aunt, and he won't keep me away from her."

Mr. Penny smiled and patted her on the back. "I thought you might say that. The nurse told me since she has her own room, we can all go in. You want to come with us, Ben?"

Ben looked at Coral for her approval. She nodded.

Coral spent the rest of the night watching the machines that monitored her aunt's blood pressure and heart rate. Leaning against the bed railing, she fell in and out of sleep until she sat up and checked her phone for an email from Tara. She found nothing and decided to update her.

Aunt Ruby has been in a car accident. She's in the hospital right now with a broken foot and a sprained shoulder. I'm in the room with her, and she's hooked up to all these machines. It looks like she's sleeping, but she's in a coma. There might be brain damage. They aren't sure. I'll update you as soon as I know more. Pray for us.

There was a bruise developing across her aunt's forehead. The gash was glued shut. Under the thin blanket covering her, Coral could see that her arm was in a sling and her foot was wrapped up. Her chest went up and down regularly, so her breathing was strong. She looked as if she could wake up anytime, just like Snow White, but Aaron wasn't her Prince Charming. Coral leaned back against the bed railing and listened to the machines, determined not to fall asleep.

***

No one in the room noticed Ned taking pictures because they had all dozed off, including the man who was now claiming to be Ruby's fiancé. It would be a brief engagement. Next time he would make sure she wasn't breathing. He took a close-up shot of Coral with her glasses resting on her nose like an old woman. Without those glasses and her awkward teenage demeanor, she'd be stunning. Those metal frames made her look like a doctor. Ned never dated educated women because they asked too many questions. But for the right one, he'd make an exception.

***

The light of a new day crept slowly into the peach-colored room, awakening Coral. She couldn't believe she'd fallen into a dreamless sleep again. What if her aunt had reached out in some way and she missed it? Slowly stretching, she sat up. Everyone was still asleep, so she checked her phone. No response from Tara.

From the corner of her eye, she saw movement. Hopeful, she pinned her eyes on her aunt. Her hand jerked encouragingly. Coral got to her feet. Aunt Ruby's body moved slowly from top to bottom like a crowd wave at a sports game. Coral froze, ready to scream if it was a seizure. All she could hear were the machines and her heart pounding in those few long moments while nothing else happened. She sank heavily back into her chair and searched for the nurse's call button.

Her aunt's eyes suddenly fluttered. Coral held her breath. Then they opened, meeting hers. She pulled off her oxygen mask and in a raspy voice asked, "Where are we?"

"The hospital. You were in a car accident, and you have a broken foot and sprained shoulder."

Ben jumped from his sleeping spot to stand next to Coral. Mr. Penny and Aaron were still asleep.

Aunt Ruby shook her head and cleared her throat. Coral offered her some water. Her aunt gave a tiny smile and held up a finger as she sipped through the straw. "I don't remember being in an accident. I know I got your snorkeling sets rented. I looked for some binoculars, but there weren't any. I was on the way back to the hotel, then—nothing."

"A truck hit your car, but they haven't caught the driver yet."

Mr. Penny, awakened by their voices, rose and stood next to the bed. "We were so worried about you, Ruby, but I should have known nothing could hurt that hard head of yours."

"Nothing," Aunt Ruby confirmed, attempting another smile.

"I'll get the nurse."

"Thanks, Ben. I'm going to call Sarah. She'll be over the moon to hear you're awake."

"Tell her hello for me, Robert. Coral, I'm sorry to have scared you." Aunt Ruby's voice cracked.

"You never have to apologize for an accident to people who love you." Aaron abruptly appeared by the bedside and grasped Aunt Ruby's hand. "I'm sorry this happened to you. I thought I had lost you this time—after just finding you."

"I'm not going anywhere." Aunt Ruby sat up with a grimace. "I don't want this to ruin your vacation, either."

"It's not ruined if you're okay. I—"

"Yes, Coral is right. Nothing is ruined," Aaron interrupted. Coral held back an eye roll. "Wherever you are is where I want to be. I'll not leave your side until they discharge you. I promise. Coral, you must be exhausted."

"I'm fine." He wouldn't be getting rid of her that easily.

Ruby held her gaze. "Yes, you should go back to the hotel and get some sleep. Then go ahead and do all the things Mrs. Penny planned for you. Besides being sore, I feel fine. Don't worry."

"I'm not worried now that you're out of your coma." Coral added a smile.

"A coma? That was just a good night's sleep, right, Aaron?" Aunt Ruby winked.

"Of course, Ruby. You look like the princess who was woken by her true love's kiss." His voice was syrupy. It ground against her nerves like the screech of worn-out brakes.

"Thank you." Aunt Ruby blushed.

"The doctor will be in soon." Ben breathlessly announced.

"Thanks." Coral was happy he was there.

He placed his hand on her shoulder. "No problem."

She felt a pleasant jolt surge through her. It was that thing she noticed between Mr. and Mrs. Penny—that spark. That was what was lacking between her aunt and Aaron. He was all talk and nothing beyond that. Her aunt would see that soon. She was sorry that Aunt Ruby would be hurt, but she'd be glad to get rid of him in the end. She was too good for a man like him.

Aaron lavished more meaningless compliments on Aunt Ruby until the doctor finally arrived.

Dr. Lee confirmed, in a surprised tone, what was obvious to everyone: she was fine.

"We'll run a few more tests, and you'll spend one more night here for observation and your results. I think you'll be going home tomorrow, Ms. Hyde. I recommend a local place that rents wheelchairs since crutches would hurt that shoulder right now. I'll check in later." He handed Mr. Penny a card and rushed out of the room.

"Thank you, Doctor," Aunt Ruby called and then turned her attention to Coral. "Get some sleep. I'm sure they will do every test they can think of before I get to leave. You should make the Hana trip tomorrow." She smiled at Aaron.

Aaron stroked her hair. "I think it's a good plan for Coral and the Pennys to carry on tomorrow. I'll be here to take care of your every need. No worries."

Mr. Penny crossed his arms. "Let's get through today and see what the next day brings. I agree with getting Coral and Ben back to the hotel for some rest. I'll keep in close contact with the hospital. We'll be back in a couple of hours, Ruby." He tucked his Hawaiian shirt back into his pants where it had come loose. Mrs. Penny wasn't there to tell him that wasn't how you wore them.

"Thank you for watching over her, Robert."

"Anytime. She's family to us. Just like you are." Mr. Penny threw a hard look at Aaron.

"I'll see you later, Aunt Ruby. I love you." Coral carefully hugged her.

"I love you too. You know, I feel surprisingly well for someone who's been in a car accident and a coma. Maybe the drugs they have in me are really good."

Ben and Mr. Penny also hugged her goodbye. "I guess you're staying. We'll relieve you later, Aaron."

"No need. I don't plan on leaving her side." Aaron beamed at Aunt Ruby as he rubbed her cheek.

"Bye." She quickly left the room but overheard Aaron telling her not to talk anymore because she needed her rest. Coral shuddered.

Chapter 15
Underwater World

The minute the taxi pulled away from the hospital, Coral's eyes shut in a dreamless sleep. She woke to Ben gently shaking her—they were at the hotel already. She declined the Pennys' offer to join them for breakfast. All she wanted to do was climb into bed and sleep.

"I'll walk you to your room." Ben walked ahead, not waiting for her response.

She heard Mr. Penny's door shut right as they got to her room.

"Do you want company? We never finished our conversation."

"I'm so tired, and I'm afraid I'd just fall asleep on you. The only thing I have to add is that I'm not out of your league." Coral blushed.

"I—well, thanks for responding to one of my dumber moments. I know you need to sleep, so I'll wait here until you're safely inside." Ben stepped closer to her, and their eyes met.

Her heart took off as he leaned in. In response she tilted her head up as she closed out the world. He gently brushed his lips over hers for a few seconds until she wrapped her arms around his neck and returned a kiss that ended as quickly as it started. Breathless, she leaned her head on his warm chest and melted into his arms. In that small window of bliss, the horror of the day was forgotten. She felt safe.

He finally pulled back from her, staring into her eyes.

I could easily get lost in those eyes.

Then he took her card for the lock and opened her door. He stepped inside and pulled her into another embrace. They held on to each other in silence before he whispered in her ear, "I've wanted to do that the whole trip, Coral, but . . . You aren't mad at me that I did it now, are you?"

Coral pulled back with a small smile. "Quite the opposite."

He exhaled loudly. "Good. I'd never want to do anything to hurt you. I want you to understand that. You're important to me." He wore the same expression she had seen on Mr. Penny when he looked at his wife. It scared her a little.

"You're important to me too. I, um . . . should get some sleep. I imagine your sister is probably wondering where you are."

He brushed his hand against her cheek, kissed the top of her head, and set her key card down. "Sleep well, Coral. Don't worry. Your aunt will be okay. And we'll deal with Aaron together." He smiled one last time before shutting the door behind him.

Coral was too exhausted to process what had happened other than to know she was happy about it. She sent off a quick email letting Tara know that her aunt had woken up from the coma and seemed fine. She'd explain the rest later. She climbed into bed without changing, and the roar of the ocean lulled her into a deep sleep.

***

The dream began as it normally did, and she arrived at the cave. As her eyes adjusted, she was amazed by the beauty—the houses, tall buildings, and gold paths. A large group of people were walking toward her on a long, golden dock. The dolphin left, and she was floating in the water waiting—

Ring. Ring. Ring.

The phone interrupted her dream again. She sat up and grabbed the receiver. "Hello?"

She heard her aunt's familiar voice. "I wanted to make sure you were okay. Mrs. Penny said you haven't left the room. Are you still sleeping? It's after one. Robert and Ben got up an hour ago."

"I'm up. I was getting ready to call the Pennys. Meet up for lunch."

"Good. I didn't want to wake you, but I guess I was worried about you."

"I'm fine, and I'd want to talk to you whether I was asleep or not, but I wasn't. Don't worry."

"I'll always worry about you, Coral. It's my job." Aunt Ruby chuckled. Coral forced a laugh, and her aunt continued. "Mrs. Penny said she'd bring you here to visit later. The rental place already replaced the car. Good service, I'd say."

"It is."

"Well, I should let you get ready. I'll see you soon. Love you."

"Love you too, and I can't wait to see you. Bye."

It had been good to hear Aunt Ruby's voice. Someday she'd see who was in her dream. She hadn't had the second dream once on this vacation, and she realized it didn't matter anymore. Her stomach rumbled, reminding her that sleep wasn't the only thing she needed.

She hopped in the shower to wash away the previous day's stress and her lingering need to sleep. The warm water rushed down, soothing her body but not her mind. She couldn't get the image of her aunt in the hospital bed out of her head.

I can't lose anyone else.

At least one good thing had happened to her this vacation—Ben. The thought of the kiss brought a smile to her face as she shut off the shower. She put on a new dress Mrs. Penny had bought her, ran a brush through her hair, and then added mascara and lipstick. Her reflection in the mirror satisfied her.

Someone gently knocked on her door, and she pulled it open. Ben waltzed in carrying a bag. The twinkle in his eyes gave her stomach butterflies.

"We ate lunch, so my mom ordered you a burger for when you woke up." He handed her the bag with a small shrug.

"Thank you. I'm starving."

"You're welcome. Um, do you want company while you eat? Or I could go." Ben wiped his palms on his shorts and glanced at the ocean.

Coral sank in to the couch. "I would like you to stay, unless . . . " She suddenly wasn't hungry. "You don't regret what happened earlier, do you?"

"Regret it? Nope. I was just being polite. Do you? Regret it?"

"Nope. Would you stop being polite? It's making me nervous. Sit down."

He sat next to her. "If you insist. You know you can heat your burger in the microwave." He pointed.

"Nah, it's good the way it is. Thanks for bringing it to me." Coral smiled, unwrapped the burger, and then took a big bite.

Ben put his arm around her. "I hardly slept, did you?"

"I just woke up."

"Did you, well, did you dream again?" He looked out at the ocean.

"Yes, I did. The phone woke me up, so I didn't get to finish it, but I saw a city made of gold and people walking toward me."

"Wow! That sounds cool. I wonder who the people were."

"No idea. Maybe I'll get to find out."

"Hope so." Ben extended his long legs and put his feet on the table.

Coral finished her burger quickly as they sat in comfortable silence. "You know I was supposed to set you up with Tara this vacation."

"Tara? Your friend? Very pretty, but not my type, you know. Not like you are." Ben grinned and grabbed one of her fries.

"Well, that's good because she already found a new boyfriend in New York."

"Perfect. You know, I've liked you for years. You just never noticed."

"You have? I—well, I never paid much attention until now." Coral washed her fries down with the soda.

"I've had no problem waiting."

Her pulse started racing as she shot up. No one had ever had this effect on her before. "Tara encouraged me to notice you."

"I'll have to thank her for that." He grinned and patted the couch where she had been sitting.

Coral sank back down next to him. "Um, what is everyone else doing?"

"My mom and Beth are getting some things for your aunt, and my dad is picking up a wheelchair. I volunteered to bring your meal to you." Ben laid his head on top of hers.

"So it's just the two of us?" Coral plopped the last french fry in her mouth and washed it down with the rest of her root beer. She looked up at him. He smiled and kissed her again. This was something she could get used to.

He jumped from the couch when the phone rang.

She answered it. "No one there."

"Weird."

"They'll call back if it's important. When are we going back to the hospital?"

"Later. They're doing tests all day, Dad said. So I thought it might be good to swim for a while. If that's okay with you?" Ben grabbed her hand.

"Swim? It's kind of weird to have fun with my aunt in the hospital, but I know she's going to be okay and home soon." Coral squeezed his hand. It was warm and strong.

"It's up to you."

There was so much caring in his expression it felt like an ocean of calmness was washing over her. "Well, maybe we could take some pictures and show her. You know, so she won't worry about me like she does."

"Good idea. I rented snorkels for you, me, and Beth this morning. I have no idea what happened to the ones your aunt rented. You'll like snorkeling, and like my sister said, you should learn how to scuba dive. We can do that in Lake Tahoe, you know."

"I'd like to learn."

"Cool. And Coral, don't tell Beth I said anything, but she's always trying to impress you. You know she looks up to you?"

"No idea why." Coral laughed.

"Cause you're you." Ben's eyes were so intense she felt like she could see his soul.

"Oh, that explains it. I, um, gotta, get my suit on, so grab the snorkel stuff. They'll be back soon?"

"Should be. I'll meet you in the hall."

"Sure."

Ben hugged her and left. Coral was amazed at how their relationship had changed overnight and couldn't wait to see where it would go. She was humming as she pulled on her sparkly blue swimsuit.

As soon as she stepped out the door, Beth and Mrs. Penny arrived, with Ben carrying several big bags into their room. Mr. Penny was right behind them with a wheelchair.

"We'll meet you kids downstairs!" Mrs. Penny called from their room. Coral and Ben sat in separate chairs on the balcony, waiting for Beth to change. Ben winked at her, and she wondered how Beth would feel if she knew.

The elevator ride down was quiet. It was uncomfortable with Beth watching them. They met up with Mr. and Mrs. Penny in the lobby and headed to the beach. Mr. and Mrs. Penny found two empty lounge chairs under a big umbrella while Ben, Beth, and Coral set down their towels on the hot sand.

"Look. There's a turtle!" Beth pointed in the direction of a large group of people.

"Let's go see it." Ben finished putting lotion on his shoulders.

Beth shook her head. "After Coral gets my back. I don't wanna burn. I can get yours too, Coral."

By the time they had both been safely covered in sunscreen, the turtle had retreated into the sea. "There's more out there." Beth grabbed her fins.

Ben was spraying their face masks with a baby shampoo solution that would keep them from fogging up. Coral slipped hers on and adjusted it, following Ben's example.

At the water's edge, she put on her fins and awkwardly hobbled into the warm ocean water with her waterproof camera safely around her neck. There was no easy or graceful way to do it with fins on, but finally she got out far enough to sink into the water and swim. Ben and Beth were right next to her. When they got past the splashing swimmers, they put their snorkels in. On their right side was the cliff people dove from, so they stayed out far enough to avoid it.

Coral was disappointed at first. She thought she'd see a ton of fish, but she only saw people's legs and rocks, like on Oahu. They swam to where everyone else was going, just around the cliff to the cove under their hotel room. She got water in her snorkel, coughed, uprighted herself, and blew it out. She adjusted her mask and caught up to Beth, who was waiting for her. Ben was already around the corner.

Turning the corner, they saw fish off to their right. Coral took a picture, and they darted away. Up ahead was a group of people around a large turtle, and she was able to get two good shots before it dove deep into the water under them. Ben came up beside her and tapped her arm, pointing. A group of rocks with some coral was surrounded by yellow-and-black fish, with blue-and-green fish swimming off to the side. Coral kept snapping pictures of the fish and rocks, but she got a couple of shots of Ben and Beth underwater too.

Ben and Beth were looking at the sea anemones that reminded her of wildflowers when a turtle came up to her. She snapped a shot of it. She couldn't believe no one else was around. Then she flashed back to her dream.

Is this the same turtle?

Did it just nod to her? No, it couldn't have, but part of her expected to be pulled under like her dream. Suddenly the turtle was gone, and a scuba diver swam past her, giving a thumbs up. He had a camera. Ben tapped on her arm and pointed up, and they surfaced to talk.

"You should see the fish and pink coral over there. It's amazing."

"A turtle was just next to me."

"Like your dream?" Ben asked with a slight frown.

"Yes, it did look like it, but it left, and I'm still here," Coral teased.

"I hope nothing takes you away from me." Ben's voice was barely above a whisper.

"Not my plan. Oh, I saw a scuba diver, and he had a camera, and I know we do too, but . . . "

"Yeah, divers take pictures too, but the way things have been going, keep an eye out for him, and I will too. Let's go find Beth."

Beth surfaced next to them. "Get water in your mask? I hate that part."

"Yeah, I've sucked in the water a couple of times," Coral admitted.

"I don't like that either. But today's been fun, right?"

"Right," Coral agreed.

Beth pointed. "I think there's a turtle over there that everyone is looking at. Come on."

"Oh, cool."

"Let's go." Ben adjusted his mask.

The turtle swimming around the crowd wasn't her turtle. Still, she snapped another couple of shots of it and then of Ben and Beth. She even took a selfie, which she wasn't a fan of, to show Aunt Ruby and maybe Tara. They chased a few more fish around but didn't see anything else, including the scuba diver. Soon they were heading back to shore after seeing another school of yellow-and-black fish that looked like the angelfish at the pet store.

Coral quickly showered and put her orange-and-red sundress back on. She loved their new room with all the colorful tropical-flower décor and the view of the palms against the ocean. With ten minutes to spare before she met the Pennys to go to the hospital, she glanced around the room for something her aunt might want. Her extra glasses—she hadn't seen them at the hospital—toothbrush, makeup bag, bathrobe, nightgown, a sundress and underthings, and flip-flops.

She checked her phone and found an email from Tara: *I am so glad your aunt is OK! We're praying for a quick recovery. Keep us updated. My mom and dad send their love. Love you!*

No time to update her relationship status. Coral rushed out the door with her beach bag full of her aunt's things and the room key. The minute she got to the car, she saw Ben. His smile had a wonderfully soothing effect on her. Okay, she was starting to think like those sappy movies now. She smiled back and climbed in between him and Beth. She closed her eyes, shutting out Beth's sly grin, and soon fell asleep.

Chapter 16
The Woman in the Dream

The ride went fast, and she woke up lying on Ben's shoulder. She quickly sat up, and Beth winked at her. Soon they were walking into Aunt Ruby's room.

"Hello!" Aaron stood up from the metal chair next to Aunt Ruby's bed.

"Hi, everyone." Aunt Ruby adjusted her bed so she was sitting up.

"How are you, dear?" Mrs. Penny leaned over to kiss her.

"I have a few bumps and bruises, but I feel myself." Aunt Ruby gave everyone a tired smile.

Coral hugged her aunt while Aaron looked on with a chilling smirk. She wished he would leave.

"I love orange on you, Coral." Aunt Ruby reached out and grabbed her hand. "I hope everyone is still having fun. I insist, you know."

Coral shrugged. "I've been worried about you, but I knew you'd worry if I didn't do something vacationy. So we snorkeled, and I got some pictures—which I forgot."

"I can see them later. Tell me about it."

"Well, there were a couple of turtles, which was my favorite part. There were some cool fish but not until we got around that cliff. I hope we can go snorkeling together soon, and I wouldn't mind taking some scuba lessons too." Coral smiled.

"I'll take the lessons with you!"

Aaron pushed next to Coral. "Until you're fully healed, you won't be doing anything but resting, sweetheart. And Coral, there's never any need to worry when I'm here. Glad you kids had some fun." He put his hand on her aunt's shoulder, making Coral want to peel it off of her.

"You've taken good care of me, Aaron, thank you. I'm sorry to have scared everyone, though." Aunt Ruby dropped Coral's hand and took Aaron's.

"Don't apologize for being in an accident." Mr. Penny shook his head at her. "The person who should apologize is the one who hit you."

"Yes, I agree." Mrs. Penny nodded, pursing her lips.

"I'm glad you didn't visit earlier today. They had me doing tests that took hours. Poor Aaron had to sit around and wait for me." Ruby gazed at him like an adoring teenager.

"No place I'd rather be than with you." He kissed her cheek while glancing up at Coral.

"Yes, we made sure the kids swam today because of all the testing." Mrs. Penny settled into a chair. "Plus, we got your wheelchair and things I thought you might need. I got you some clothes to wear home, magazines, and stuff."

"Oh, yeah!" Coral remembered and held up the beach bag, "I brought your extra glasses, your bathrobe, nightgown, clothes, and your toothbrush."

"You guys are too good to me. Thank you, Sarah and Robert. Good thinking, Coral—my glasses are bent and have a crack in them." She held them up.

"Of course."

Mr. Penny was studying Aaron, who smiled back, although it seemed more like a challenge.

Aunt Ruby yawned widely. "Sorry. Today was a long day. You don't get much rest in a hospital."

"I'll make sure you get plenty of rest when you get back to the hotel. I had them set up my room for the wheelchair. Maybe your aunt should stay with me so I can watch over her. Do you mind, Coral?" Aaron asked with a slight grin and a raised eyebrow.

"I don't—" Coral started but was cut off by her aunt.

"I mind. I don't like the thought of Coral staying alone in a hotel room. I'll stay in my room, Aaron. Thank you for being so thoughtful, though."

Mrs. Penny held up a hand. "I'll keep an eye on Coral while you're here. We'll help with your care, don't worry."

A nurse entered. "I have your dinner for you." He set it on the tray and quickly left the room without waiting to see if anything else was needed.

"Can't say I'm not disappointed, but I completely understand. Here, I'll help you eat." Aaron picked up the plate of noodles, chicken, broccoli, and chocolate pudding.

"I can do it." Aunt Ruby shook her head.

"Nonsense. That's why I'm here."

Aunt Ruby yawned again but didn't argue. Although the room was big and private, it felt small and claustrophobic, like a packed elevator. Coral stole a glance at Ben, who was laser-focused on Aaron. Beth and Mrs. Penny were quietly double-checking their list of things Aunt Ruby would need the next day, while Mr. Penny seemed uncomfortable and kept adjusting his loud, flowered shirt. At least it was untucked now that Mrs. Penny was there.

It was awkward watching Aaron feed her aunt like she was a child. When she tried to join the conversation, he'd shove another bite of food into her mouth. Amazingly, she didn't choke, and her plate was soon empty. Her helpful boyfriend removed the tray and placed it outside the door like they were in a hotel.

"I think all she needs is a good night's sleep," he announced.

"Yes, I believe you're right, Aaron. I'll stay here until she falls asleep, and you can take this break and get some real food and a nap." Mr. Penny's tone left no room for disagreement.

"Oh, yes, Aaron, you should. Big day tomorrow." Ruby yawned again.

"Oh, I don't know about leaving you, Ruby—"

"She won't be alone. I insist." Mr. Penny's smile couldn't hide his uncompromising stare.

"Well, I could use a change of clothes and perhaps a meal other than hospital food, but I'll be back soon. Anything I can bring you?"

"There is nothing I can think of right now. Thanks, Aaron. You've done so much for me already. Not sure how I can repay you."

Aaron gave a lopsided grin. "You can repay me by taking care of yourself. Heal up. I'll do the rest. And if you feel the need to repay me, well . . . " He didn't state the obvious, and Coral was glad. He was obnoxious.

Aunt Ruby giggled and blushed at Aaron before turning her attention to Mrs. Penny, whose disgusted expression was leaking through her pleasant mask. "You're going to Hana still tomorrow, right, Sarah?"

"I'm not sure after all that's happened."

"I insist you go. Aaron's offered to bring me back to the hotel, so there's no reason not to."

"Well, I guess we could." She looked at Mr. Penny.

"If all goes well tonight." Mr. Penny grabbed his wife's hand.

"Good, it's settled. From what I understand, I won't get released until after lunch. By the time you get back, I'll be all settled in my room. The offer still stands, right, Aaron?" Aunt Ruby grinned.

"You never have to question if I'll be there for you, sweetheart." He shook his finger at her. Coral shuddered.

Ruby wrinkled her nose at him with a huge grin. "Thank you."

Mrs. Penny hugged Aunt Ruby. "Well, we should go and let you rest. See you tomorrow. If you need us, we're a phone call away."

"Be right back." Aaron winked at Aunt Ruby, making her blush.

Coral, Beth, and Ben followed Mrs. Penny out of the room after goodbyes.

Aaron walked next to Mrs. Penny, giving her a winning smile every time she looked his way. Coral knew there was nothing winning about it—if only she could prove it.

"You wouldn't mind if I took Coral out for some ice cream after dinner, would you? I'd love to spend more time with her while her aunt is in the hospital." Aaron never took his gaze off Coral while he waited for the answer.

Mrs. Penny studied him for a moment. "I think that's a good idea, and I hope you don't mind if we join you."

A shadow passed over his face for a moment, giving Coral goosebumps, "That's a great idea, Sarah. I'd love to have your company."

"In fact, why don't you join us for dinner?" Mrs. Penny asked.

Aaron smiled, but his eyes were darting side to side. "I'd love to, but I think I would like to take a nap first and get cleaned up before I go back to the hospital. Maybe I spoke too soon. Can I take a rain check on the ice cream? I'm missing Ruby already, and I want to relieve Mr. Penny so he can get home to eat. The hospital food isn't very good, I've learned."

"Don't worry about relieving him. He has an iron gut, as he'd say. He won't mind eating the food at the hospital. But I understand you want to get back. Call me if you change your mind. You have my phone number, right?" Mrs. Penny unlocked the car.

"Yes, I have your number on my cell phone." Aaron hustled to his rented red convertible. "I'll see you tomorrow. I hope you enjoy your day, and don't worry about Ruby. I'll take good care of her. Night."

"Night. See you tomorrow." Mrs. Penny slid into the driver's seat. Aaron closed his car door and quickly left. Mrs. Penny frowned, her dislike apparent. No way was she going to get ice cream or anything else with him, Coral decided. If only she could forbid her aunt, but she knew Aunt Ruby would do what she wanted. Stubborn ran in their family.

It was an uneventful ride back. Everyone seemed lost in their thoughts. Coral declined all invitations of movies or company after an equally hushed dinner filled with small talk.

Mrs. Penny hugged her. "I'll call you when it's time to get up. I'll order sandwiches for the drive. All you need is some sunscreen, your bathing suit, a change of clothes, a towel, and maybe a light wrap. I'll provide the rest. You need anything now?"

"No, I'm fine. I'm going straight to bed. It's been a long day." Coral offered a bright smile.

Ben entered the room behind Beth. He gave her an intense look and a nod, which Coral acknowledged with a small grin.

"Okay, dear. Everything has worked out perfectly, and your aunt will be back to herself in no time. Sleep well."

"Thanks."

Beth ran out after her. "Sure you don't want company? I can come over."

Coral saw Ben standing at their door, knowing he had the same idea. "I'm going right to sleep. Thanks for the offer. I'll see you guys in the morning." She stepped into her room and locked the door behind her.

She got the packing out of the way for the Hana drive and eyed the balcony. It would be a perfect night to watch the ocean and think about everything, but instead, she climbed into bed. She was asleep immediately.

***

The dream came quickly. She was pulled underwater, and soon they entered a cave. It only took a few seconds for her vision to clear. Coral shook her head as the dolphin left her treading water. The golden city made her think of ancient Rome. There were gardens in all the colors of the rainbow. She started to swim to the dock as the group of people approached.

She felt no fear. The word "merfolk" came to mind as the group drew closer. They were all exotic looking, and she saw many different shades of skin, just like in her world. Was this Atlantis? She squinted without her glasses, trying to see their faces, but they all had on matching hats, round and green, that shaded their faces. It was disappointing not to be able to see past those hats.

Canoes with no one in them floated around her. A large blue bird flew above her and dove into the water. She reached the dock. The dolphin returned and gently nudged her like it was encouraging her to get out. Then it dove into the clear, aqua liquid. She looked around for the turtle but didn't see it. The bird had not resurfaced, so that left her floating alone, waiting for the people.

Finally they were almost close enough to see their faces. Coral bravely pulled herself onto the dock but left her feet dangling in the water—just in case. Some of the faces became visible, but she didn't recognize anyone, but then there was a face that looked a lot like—

***

Ring, Ring

"No! Why does this keep happening? Stupid phone." Coral rolled over, ready to throw the shrilling phone. She sighed loudly.

"Hello?"

"Morning, Coral. I hope I didn't wake you."

"Oh, no. I was lying in bed listening to the ocean." She felt guilt course through her. A glance at the clock showed it was seven. "I haven't heard from the Pennys yet."

"I'm sure Sarah will be calling soon. I wanted to tell you to have fun today and let you know that all my tests came back negative. Besides a broken foot and bruised shoulder, I'm good to go. I feel so much better this morning and can't wait to get out of here."

"I wish you were going with us." Coral swiped the sleep from her eyes.

"I'll miss being with you, but I want you to see the sights. Besides, I've done the Hana drive before. It's your first Hawaiian vacation—I don't want you to worry about me. I'm fine. One more day of rest, and I'll be ready to hang out with you tomorrow at the pool, okay?"

"Okay," Coral agreed, and then she heard a voice in the background.

Aunt Ruby continued. "Aaron wants you to know he'll be here all day. Don't forget the sunscreen, and take lots of pictures. Love you."

"Love you too." Coral hung up.

The Pennys wouldn't be far behind, so she headed to the shower and had just finished brushing her teeth when there was a knock at the door. Coral opened it to find Beth, who was dressed in another new tropical dress— yellow this time. She had on bright pink lipstick, which brought out her blue eyes, and her brown hair was braided, as it always was. She was ready to go.

"Mom sent me over. I guess your phone was busy when she called. She's been up since six. I have too. Ben woke me up when he left the room to swim with Dad." She grinned.

"That sucks." Coral thought about telling her about her new feelings for Ben but decided to wait.

"Mom told me to tell you it would be better to wear your swimsuit under your clothes and bring a towel. She suggested a change of clothes, and you won't need your snorkel stuff today. It'll be just a quick swim. Are you ready, or should I wait?"

"I should only be a few minutes. I'll meet you in your room, if that's okay?"

A wave of disappointment crossed Beth's face, but she quickly covered it with a huge fake smile. "Sure. I'll leave the door ajar so you can come right in. I guess I'll see where Dad and Ben are. I thought you could go with me if you were ready, but, well, you aren't, and you still have to eat. I'm fairly sure Mom ordered every breakfast item from the menu, so help yourself."

Coral forced a laugh. "Thanks, Beth. It won't take me long."

"Don't rush. We don't have to leave right away because my dad and Ben haven't eaten either. Do you know Ben asked if I wanted to go swimming with them? Before sunrise? Crazy. See you in a few." Beth bolted down the carpeted hall to the elevator.

105

D. L. Finn

Chapter 17
Hana Drive

Coral allowed herself a few moments of reflection and looking at the ocean after she slipped a sundress printed with her new favorite flower—plumeria—over her swimsuit. The yellow, white, and pink flowers with the heavenly scent were abundant on the islands, and their sweetness drifted up from the gardens below. Yet it was her dream that tugged on her attention more than the pleasing fragrance. It was disappointing that the face in her dream hadn't belonged to one of her parents, but the older woman seemed familiar in that dreamlike way. Maybe tonight she'd find out more.

She shot off a quick update to Tara:

Aunt Ruby is doing better. All her tests came back good, and they're releasing her later today. Aaron suggested she stay in his room so he can take care of her. Thankfully, she told him no. Can you believe him? I mean, they've only been dating a few days. The guy's a creep, but it doesn't look like we're getting rid of him anytime soon. You'll see what I mean when you meet him since he lives near us.

Anyways, here's where you get to hear how right you were—so enjoy it. Ben and I are together now. We still have a lot to talk about, and I'm not sure how Beth will take it. I might tell her today when we go on the Hana drive. It's supposed to take all day. I'll send you some pictures later and keep you updated.

Oh, I almost forgot that I finally got to see what was in that cave in my dream—a golden city. It was beautiful. Many people were coming to me when an older woman stepped out of the group, like the leader. Anyway, I got woken up before they spoke to me. Maybe tonight I'll finally talk to them.

107

I love and miss you, Tara. Can't wait to see you. Sending love back to your family.

"Turtle!" someone called out right as Coral hit send. She watched the commotion below, wishing to be a part of that group. Too bad the Pennys had a long day planned and snorkeling wasn't on the itinerary. As she rechecked her bag and glanced around the room, the feeling that she had forgotten something was strong.

Out of habit her hand went to her neck, but she didn't find her necklace. Once she had it and the matching earrings and bracelet back in place, she headed over to the Pennys. Soon her plate was full of fruit, eggs, bacon, and toast. She was still eating when Beth and Mr. Penny entered.

"Good morning, Coral. I hope you don't mind that we took an early morning swim without you. We thought you might need some extra sleep." Mr. Penny laid his towel over a chair.

"Morning," Coral mumbled with a full mouth and added, "No problem." Mr. Penny left to change.

"Ben's getting dressed." Beth smiled and grabbed a muffin.

Coral nodded and went back to eating. She was done when Ben rushed into the room. He smiled at Coral, and she returned it with Beth's eyes pinned on them. A frown passed over Beth's face, and Coral felt disappointment course through her. She had kind of hoped Beth would be pleased and decided not to say anything today.

She glanced at the clock. It was seven forty-five when Mrs. Penny finally emerged from the bedroom with a coffee cup in hand.

"Did you get enough to eat, Coral? I'm sorry I wasn't here to greet you. I was applying sunscreen. I don't like to get sunburned—it ages you. Anyways, the hotel delivered our lunch in an ice bag." Mrs. Penny pointed to a blue padded bag like the one her aunt used when they bought groceries.

"I got plenty, thank you."

Ben and his dad piled their plates high with breakfast goodies that they promptly devoured. They were all ready and on the road by eight fifteen.

It was a quiet start for the Penny family. Beth, perched between Coral and Ben in the back seat, was unusually silent. The middle seat was loaded down with all their stuff. The mood was heavy. Aunt Ruby's accident weighed on all of them, even though she was going to be okay.

Coral caught Ben studying her more than once over his sister. Why had she left her cell phone in her bag? They could be texting right now. Beth focused on her phone while Ben appeared to be reading, but Coral never saw him turn an electronic page. The Pennys chatted quietly about the drive and where they would stop, a conversation Beth was usually involved in. Not this time, though.

Coral closed her eyes, peeking out occasionally to see where they were. She wished they'd waited to make this trip, but her aunt had been insistent that they go and probably wouldn't be comfortable on the long drive, even later. She sighed gently. At least she was finally going to the place where her parent's plane had crashed. It felt surreal.

They drove through a small town and were soon on the narrow, curvy road Beth had warned her about. Coral sat up and looked out her window. She trusted Mr. Penny's driving, though, and wasn't that concerned about the cliffs below them.

Finally the subdued group came to their first stop. Ben let his sister out, and she took off to catch up to her parents, leaving them alone at last. Coral glanced around, making sure they weren't the subject of anyone's photography, and grabbed her phone and camera to take some pictures.

"You'll like this bamboo forest. It's pretty cool."

Beth looked back and waved. She was sure throwing some confusing signals when it came to her brother.

"Wanna pose over by that tree?"

"I'm not one for taking pictures." Ben lowered his voice. "But for you, I will."

Coral snapped some quick shots of Ben, who stood in front of the thick forest with his arms dangling by his side like they were numb. At least he smiled.

"Okay, you next." He snatched the camera from her.

Coral laughed. "Hey, I'm the photographer here."

Ben pointed, and she walked over and smiled. After a few shots, he seemed satisfied.

Beth had come back to them. "You two stand over here. I'll take another picture."

Neither bothered protesting as they stood awkwardly next to each other. Mr. Penny came back. "Sorry we got ahead of you guys. Let me take a picture of the three of you. Smile now."

D. L. Finn

Ben brushed up against her, and it felt like she had been struck by lightning. *Talk about the guy being right in front of you the whole time.* They caught up to Mrs. Penny, who was sitting on a bench.

"Would you be a dear, Coral, and take a picture of our whole family?" Mrs. Penny asked. "I forgot my camera in the car."

"No problem." Coral shot several pictures of the happy Penny family. In the end she zoomed in on Ben and took one extra shot for herself. She smiled. "Got it."

"Good. I always like to record all our good times together. Oh, we should get one of all the kids."

"Got it already."

"Oh, good, thank you, dear. Let's get going, then. Lots to see today."

"We're almost there. Come on, everyone." Mr. Penny took the lead in his flashy blue surfing Santa shirt.

Beth came up behind Coral and whispered, "I'm glad you and my brother are getting along. I'll stay with my parents. Carry on." She ran off.

"What was that all about?" Ben asked as they started to walk behind the rest of the family.

Coral told him, and he nodded. "I wondered how she'd take that. I was going to talk to her later, but I'm not surprised she figured it out. She's a bit of a romantic." He laughed.

"I know. She's dragged me to several movies. Although right now, I wouldn't mind going to them as much. Especially with the right person," Coral blurted out before she could take it back.

"I was thinking the same thing myself. I'm glad we're both on the same page. So, you think this might be more than just a holiday fling, as they say?" Ben gave her a side glance and then winked.

Coral did her best not to laugh at "holiday fling." *Bet he got that from his sister.* "I'd very much like to continue this back in real life—on a slow track, if you don't mind. That is, if that's what you want to do," she quickly added as she stumbled over a rock. Ben caught her before she fell. "Thanks."

"Slow is fine with me, and I kind of like being there for you. I mean, I'd like us both to be there for each other."

"I'd like that too." Coral blushed. She never thought she'd act so silly like this, especially over someone she'd known for so many years.

"Let's wait on telling my parents and your aunt until after vacation, okay?"

"I was thinking the same thing."

"Good. Because after that, I want everyone to know we're together. That is, if you do? I mean, you're much more popular at school than me. You go to all the events and parties. I won't be a step down for you?" His expression shifted from a frown to a smile faster than the speed of light, but Coral saw it.

"Are we going through this again? No. Tara's popular. She's always dragging me along to things I don't want to do. Most of the time, I'd rather be home reading. None of that is important to me, anyway—is it to you?"

"Sorry. I don't mean to keep bringing it up, and I won't again. I know you answered me before, but I wanted to double-check, and I promise this is the last time I bring it up. As for all that social stuff, none of it is important to me either. Never has been."

"Good. I do have one question, though—what do you read?"

Ben tilted his head. "Read? Everything. I prefer fantasy or adventure, but I'll read just about anything if I'm bored, including the cereal box at home. I kind of thought it might be weird to you how much I read."

"Weird? No! I read too. Just not all the nonfiction stuff we do at school. I read fantasy and adventure stuff too."

"My favorite book as a kid was *The Hobbit*. Now give me a dragon, elf, hobbit, or sword fight, and I'll read it." Ben laughed.

"No way! *The Hobbit* was my favorite too. How did we not know this about each other all these years?" Coral could hear the waterfall in the background. "I was thinking—"

Mrs. Penny waved. "We're here! Come on, kids. One more shot by the waterfall. No time to swim here. If we want to swim, it'll be on the black beach."

They dutifully took their pictures and headed back to the car. This time Beth walked with them, talking the entire time about the rest of the trip. Coral noticed Ben glancing back. Was someone taking their picture? She looked but didn't see anything.

The drive was supposed to take three and a half hours, but they made several stops, including a bathroom break.

Ben whispered to Coral as she came out of the bathroom. "I haven't seen anyone take our picture lately besides us, but I'll keep watching."

111

"Maybe that was just on Oahu?"

"I hope so, but don't forget Reno. I wonder—"

"Come on, Mom and Dad are already in the car," Beth called as she rushed off.

"To be continued. Let's go." Ben grinned.

"Lead the way to the Shire." Coral grinned back.

***

Behind the restrooms a camera was pointed at Ben and Coral. Ned was wearing green and blended in with the foliage. He knew they'd stop here and waited until they got into their rental before he came out and got in his car. Even though he knew where they were going, it was important not to lose sight of them. He pulled in front of a family crammed into an economy rental. The father laid on his horn. Ned waved and smiled.

"Oops, sorry!" he called to them, keeping in character.

After his assignment he hurried on to the next step, following another change of plans regarding Ruby's survival.

***

Mr. Penny crossed a one-lane bridge. He stopped at the side of the road to let them take a quick picture of some waterfalls before moving on. Coral was too focused on the amazing scenery to look for anyone taking photos of them. How she wished she and Ben could jump into the pool below them, but that wasn't her reality. They kept driving.

Chapter 18
Black Beach

"We're here!" Beth added another layer of sunscreen to her face. Coral saw the sign for Waianapanapa State Park and knew that name. It was the place her parents' plane had crashed. Mr. Penny glanced back at her in the rearview mirror with a slight frown. He remembered, but what about the rest of the family? Were they unaware, or did they not want to upset her? She went with the latter and would play along, feeling confident that today would bring her closure one way or another.

Taking a deep breath, she responded in a normal tone. "Cool."

Beth's energy seemed to increase with each word. "We're going to Pailoa Beach. It's black sand—you'll love it!"

"Don't forget the lava tube." Ben grabbed his towel and avoided looking at Coral.

Mrs. Penny put on a colorful, wide-brimmed hat. "Would you boys grab our food, please?"

Beauty spread out before them on the shiny black beach that they had almost to themselves. The waves gently caressed the sand and volcanic rocks, but Beth's voice splintered the peace. "After this we're going to explore the town of Hana and then see the seven sacred pools. Never swam in those because of water issues, but maybe someday. Then we go back the way we came. You—"

There was a splash out in the distance. Coral pointed. "Is that a dolphin?"

Beth squinted and shaded her eyes. "I don't see one. Guess I missed it. Come on. Maybe we'll see more."

They hustled down the stairs, kicked off their flip-flops, and dug their toes into the warm sand. A shiver ran through Coral—this was her Pearl Harbor. They'd only recovered the plane.

"Right here." Mrs. Penny had found the perfect spot for them to set up camp with all the stuff Ben and Mr. Penny had lugged from the parking lot.

The blue waters were calling to Coral, cutting through the melancholy of the moment. She was going to swim where her parents had taken their last breath or . . .

"Let's eat before you swim." Mrs. Penny spread out a floral blanket.

Coral wasn't hungry. Her desire to swim increased with the momentum of a breaching whale. Ben was eyeing the area where the lava tube was. She wouldn't mind exploring that with him, but she had something to do first.

Beth was helping her mother while Coral laid the towels out.

"I hope everyone has sunscreen?" Mrs. Penny adjusted her hat and cleaned her Maui Jim sunglasses. Everyone nodded.

The straps of Mrs. Penny's yellow, tropical-print, skirted bathing suit peeked from under her pineapple sundress. Mr. Penny had on matching yellow trunks. Ben's long swim trucks were green and blue with palm trees framing an orange-and-red sunset, and Beth's yellow-swirl one-piece was even more daring than her pink one, and again, it suited her.

Coral took the offered chicken sandwich and lay on her towel between Beth and Ben.

Beth smiled. "Isn't this a beautiful spot? I love coming here. It seems like it's our private place, except for them." She nodded toward a family with two toddlers playing in the sand and started nibbling on her sandwich.

"It's a great place to swim, but we should go through the lava tube first." Ben smiled.

"I'd like to explore, but would you mind swimming first?"

"If you want to. We have time to do both."

"Thanks."

"Welcome." Ben took a huge bite of his sandwich, leaving a bit of chicken on his chin. Beth quickly wiped it away and then rolled her eyes at Coral.

"The tube is wonderful, and there are more caves in this park. Maybe we can see those too if we have time." Mr. Penny finished his sandwich in one large bite.

"We'll see." Mrs. Penny carefully wiped her mouth.

Coral smiled at Ben and then tilted her head up to the cliffs. He scanned the area and shook his head. Satisfied they were photographer-free, Coral buried her feet in the warm black sand. She gobbled down her sandwich without really tasting it. Peace filled her. She smiled as she absorbed the sun's rays and made her decision. Ben would not like what she was about to do.

Ben stuffed the rest of his sandwich in his mouth and studied the ocean. Beth and Mrs. Penny was pulling out the chips, but Coral caught Mr. Penny frowning at her. Was he worried about how this beach was affecting her? She sucked down her bottle of water. Would she get her answers today?

***

Ned was perched above the group taking more pictures. He blended in nicely, like at the rest stop. All they'd see of him was the reflection of his lens. Morgan and Emerald Dover had disappeared off the radar eight years ago at this same spot. How fortunate that Coral ended up where she needed to be. There could be someone else working with his boss. He scanned the area, not seeing anyone.

An unusual tingle coursed through his body, sending a small smile to lighten his solemn working face. He'd never seen the change before but was told they looked peaceful before they got into the water. Coral looked peaceful. That had to be a good sign.

Before he flew to Maui, his boss had confided in him about a water person that came forward several years ago, thinking it was time for both worlds to meet. Unfortunately, it was mishandled by past management. What came from that encounter was a description of a gold city and the water person healing his interrogator's diabetes. The water person took his last breath in that idiot's care. The autopsy didn't shed any new light on how they breathed underwater or how the change came about in their bodies. It was as if the gills had disappeared. Ned shook his head. What a waste of a good opportunity. If they'd played it cool, the world would be a different place today, and the power would be where it belonged—with his boss.

He realized how important he must be for his boss to share that high-level information.

He adjusted his wetsuit while watching Coral sunbathe. Not that it really mattered to him, but he had to wonder why Coral's parents had left their child behind like that. Maybe water people didn't place as much importance on their children as humans did.

Ned turned his attention to Ben Penny. He hoped he wasn't going to be a problem today. He wouldn't hesitate to resolve any issues with a quick cut to the back of the ankle. That would end pursuit. Finding the city was his top priority. He started whistling and walked past Coral carrying a blue surfboard. Soon he was paddling out to the waves. He waited there for her to enter the ocean, hoping this time the change would happen.

***

Ruby was alone in the hospital, dressed and ready to be released. Aaron was still running errands. She worried about how distant he'd felt since her accident, even though his words were reassuring. Doubt was creeping in about his sincerity. But her focus was on Coral. She knew the Pennys would keep an eye on her, but she also remembered Coral's dream.

That dream had always scared Ruby. Coral claimed not to have it anymore, but Ruby wasn't sure she believed her. What if Coral tried to swim out and got a cramp or something? Ruby shivered. She couldn't wait to get out of the hospital and keep a closer eye on her niece. She couldn't lose Coral the way she'd lost her sister.

She sighed and sank back onto the hard bed right as Aaron walked in with a wheelchair. His smile washed away most of her doubts—but not all of them.

***

"Ready?" Beth jumped up.

"I am." She turned to Ben, who was brushing off sand.

"You kids be careful out there. There's no lifeguard," Mrs. Penny warned.

Mr. Penny was still frowning. Coral carefully put her glasses away and raced across the hot black sand. She dove into the clear blue water. When she came up, she saw Beth wade carefully into the water.

"Isn't this beautiful?"

"Perfect." Coral smiled. "Let's swim over to Ben."

"You guys need to check this out," Ben called off to the left.

"Coming!" Coral shouted.

She dove underwater as soon as she saw Beth heading toward her brother. She pretended to go in that direction but suddenly changed her course underwater. She held her breath and continued in the opposite direction—away from the shore. They were in a protected cove, but the pull

116

to the open sea was magnetic. She couldn't resist it. She swam hard and had gotten far before anyone noticed she wasn't headed toward Ben and Beth.

"That's too far, Coral!" Mrs. Penny shouted.

She kicked harder when she heard Ben's voice. "Wait for me, Coral!"

She took one final glance back at Mrs. Penny frantically waving her arms. Ben and Beth were headed in her direction, but Mr. Penny made no move at all. He sat on his towel with his head in his hands. Coral felt a wave of sadness. She hated leaving them behind, but she had no choice. She had to know.

Although she had a strong lead on Ben, he was gaining on her quickly. She swam even harder. She passed out of earshot of the voices telling her to come back. She kept swimming, wondering why nothing was happening. Was it all just a dream, like everyone said? Disappointment weighed her down. Perhaps it had all been wishful thinking.

Soon it would be hard for her to get back, and she almost turned around. The current was growing stronger, and she had a sudden fear that she might drown. While she paused to reconsider, Ben swam closer.

"Stop! Ignore your dream. Come back, Coral. Please! You can't do this! Don't leave me."

Coral felt a wave of peacefulness flow over her.

He won't reach you in time, a voice said in her head.

She smiled at Ben. She wasn't going to turn back. "I'm okay, Ben. Go back. It's too strong out here. I'll always—"

Just like in the dream, she was pulled under. It was starting.

She went deeper and deeper into the sea. It was getting colder, and the water was cloudy. During the first few moments, panic rushed through her about breathing, but that didn't last long as her body didn't feel air-deprived. Her legs were being tugged down into the ocean's depths. This went on longer than it had in her dream. She relaxed and let the pulling continue.

Teeth dug into her leg but didn't cause pain. She was pulled around a corner and down into a dark hole. Then they stopped. She was underwater, not knowing which way was up. They came from behind her like in her dream, a huge dolphin and a large green sea turtle. She knew what to do and got on the dolphin's back. They began to swim to a place she couldn't wait to see.

***

Mr. Penny watched Coral disappear. How would he ever explain this to Ruby? But they'd showed what they would do if he didn't cooperate. He had his wife and children to protect. Shading his eyes to scan the area for more operatives, he only saw the one he'd spotted earlier, the man who'd boldly walked past them in his wetsuit.

He knew no one would believe that Coral was riding on the back of a dolphin, hopefully not leading a team of divers to a secret cave city that held untold riches. He wasn't sure he believed any of it, even after he'd read the secret government documents after his best friend's disappearance. He squinted at his frantically waving wife. It was time to focus—for her.

He played his part and went to retrieve his panicked son and send his confused daughter back to his wife so they could call for help, not that it would matter. Mr. Penny searched with his son for close to fifteen minutes until Ben accepted that she was gone. They slowly swam back to shore.

His family gathered around him, teary-eyed. What if they learned the truth about what he did? Would he lose them by trying to protect them? The one thing that kept him going was the belief that Coral had made it back to her family the way her parents had.

***

She was living her dream—but it was different. The dolphin wasn't breaching the surface for air. Instead, they were hugging the shoreline and emerging in small caves like they were hiding. Coral frowned as they sliced through the water. She watched the turtle and dolphin exchange glances. The turtle nodded its head toward some rocks, and they took off. As soon as they got behind the rocks, they headed into a cave. Was this it? She quickly realized it wasn't.

All she wanted was to get to the cave in her dream, but something was wrong. The dolphin and turtle surfaced and angled themselves behind more rocks. She carefully peeked around the rocks just in time to see two scuba divers swimming by them. One looked like the guy she'd seen snorkeling. Three large humpback whales swam in front of the cave and blocked the view from the entrance.

The turtle swam to the closest whale and then back to them. It was clear they could communicate, and she felt left out. The dolphin blew out air and sucked in more. Then they made a quick run for the open sea with the whales protecting them. Coral held on as best she could. She almost slipped off, but the turtle was right there, pushing her back on.

They didn't slow down as they passed a large boat off to their left. In the far distance, she was sure she saw a submarine—or maybe more whales. It didn't matter because they were headed in another direction. Finally the dolphin had to surface, and the sun almost blinded Coral, just like in her dream. When her vision cleared, there weren't any boats around them. Good. The whales were suddenly gone.

They were next to a small island. She wasn't sure if it was the same one from her dream. It wasn't the same beach. The dolphin dove under the water again as they hugged the island. It made a final breach, and Coral saw what she had been dreaming for years—the familiar island shoreline. They dove again and swam toward a rocky wall. She thought they were going to crash into it when suddenly an entrance appeared. There was a light ahead, and they surfaced.

D. L. Finn

Chapter 19
Beyond the Water

The golden city was even more beautiful than her dream. The structures were Romanesque, with tall columns, but they also had a modern look. There were flowery designs, wide stairways, and welcoming doors for a contemporary flare. The rainbow trees and plants were everywhere, but the city was devoid of any activity except in the sky.

Her jaw fell open. "That's not a bird. It's a dragon."

The gentle clomping of shoes on the dock reminded her she wasn't alone. The group was coming toward her, led by the older woman. Finally she would get some answers. All she had to do was sit on the dolphin next to the turtle and wait.

Unfortunately, her companions didn't understand her plans. The dolphin suddenly dropped from underneath her and left her treading water. The turtle nodded and disappeared, leaving her alone. As she put her hand automatically to her necklace for reassurance, she felt three slits behind her ear. She had no time to wonder how they got there but was sure that was how she could breathe underwater.

Logic did not apply to her dream or to what was happening now, including seeing clearly without glasses. The cool water swirled around her as she moved her hands and feet. Should she get out or stay in case she needed to leave quickly? She stayed.

She squinted to try to make out the faces, which were mostly hidden under the same large hats she'd seen in the dream. The women had on long, flowing, cerulean skirts with what looked like abalone shells across shiny

121

white shirts, while the men were shirtless and wore baggy, turquoise pants that had swirling gold stitching. Merfolk uniforms?

"Welcome, Coral," the older woman said. She removed her hat, revealing long silver hair braided and coiled on top of her head, where a large crown of pearls rested. Her eyes were the brightest green Coral had ever seen. "My name is Sabella. I'm sorry your parents aren't here to greet you, but they're on their way."

Coral's mouth went dry. "My parents? So they're alive?"

"Of course they are. You knew that from your dreams, correct?" Sabella glanced back to the large group. The way they moved together reminded her of a school of fish, but they looked very human, like her. A large green hat nodded to the woman, causing her to smile.

"I had hoped, but . . . "

Sabella smoothed her skirt. "Well, yes, I suppose you wouldn't know what to make of anything. No one has educated you, child. Poor Ruby has forgotten us. It happens when we leave here. But I made sure you were called back strongly. Would you like to join us, or are you more comfortable where you are?"

"I'm not sure." Coral glanced around to see what else was in the water with her. Nothing but some boats that were similar to the gondolas she'd seen in pictures of the Venice canals.

"I understand. The dolphin and the turtle that helped you are nearby if you're looking for them. They helped your parents a few years ago." Sabella glanced back again.

She was different than the rest, more regal. Her blue skirt was bluer, and her pale complexion almost glowed.

A tall, muscular man with smooth skin the color of coffee pushed through the crowd bowing deeply. "Your Majesty, they're coming." He smiled brightly at Coral.

"Good, good. Thank you, General Arlo. They've been waiting for this day for a long time."

"They have, Your Majesty," General Arlo agreed. With a quick wink at Coral, he pushed his way back through the crowd.

"I should be introducing you, Coral, but you're still in the water."

It was tiring to tread water, but she stayed. "I, well . . . "

"It's okay. Be comfortable. You should know that your parents weren't happy when we brought them back without you, but it couldn't be helped.

You were always safe with your aunt before your change. Wasn't it wonderful when your gills came out?"

Coral put a hand to the strange slits on her neck. "It was strange. I have no idea how or why."

"There is no why, only that we have them. There's not always a reason for everything, like the air people try to look for. You'll learn, Coral." Sabella crossed her arms.

"I don't understand."

"I know." Sabella's face softened into a smile.

A murmur shot through the crowd, and Sabella bent to look around them. She pointed. "There they are. Maybe you'd like to come out now. I'm sure your parents would like to hug you after all these years."

Coral couldn't see, but as soon as the crowd started to part, she tentatively swam to the shiny golden dock. Remaining tense, she pulled herself out, ready to jump back in if she didn't see her parents.

A gasp caught in her throat, and she froze. Her mom and dad! Her mom looked the same. She wasn't dressed like the group. Instead, she was wearing a long red dress with black dolphins on it. Her red hair was gathered up in a bun. Her dad was wearing brown pants and a plain red shirt, very different from his usual jeans and band T-shirts or the gray suits he wore to work. His hair, always neatly groomed, had grown long like the other men's and was pulled back into a ponytail. They started to run, and Coral locked eyes with her mom.

"Coral!" Emerald cried as she pulled her into a tight hug.

"Finally." Morgan gathered them both in his arms.

Years of loss poured out of Coral. Soon they were all crying together, unable to let go.

***

Sabella studied the water. The dolphin shook its head, and she let out a sigh of relief. They'd got Coral here without being followed, thanks to the whales. That was getting harder and harder with all the air people's technology. Although that wasn't the biggest issue Sabella dealt with—the guilt of separating parents from their child had worn heavily on her for the last eight years. Even though it had been done for the good of her people, she found it excruciating. At least they were together now, even if only for a little bit. There was one more person who belonged back home: her other daughter, Princess Ruby.

She gazed warmly at her granddaughter, Coral, and daughter Emerald. Her husband, King Slate, should have never allowed their two daughters and heirs to the throne to go live in the air world. When her only son, Prince Jade, was finished with his education, her beloved husband took him to retrieve the princesses.

They'd all been too trusting. *I wanted to learn more and start interacting with the air people. Share our gifts with them, but it backfired.* Slate and Jade were made prisoners. Her husband died within days without telling them anything, and Jade cracked under the torture after his father was murdered. Those barbarians learned of their city, but not where it was. Then Jade's memories left him, and the experiments began. He died in his cell a month later, alone and scared.

She watched it happen through their eyes, unable to do anything to save them. Things had never been the same. She spent all her waking hours trying to get her daughters and granddaughter back. Nothing would be right until all her family was home. She couldn't bear to watch another child experimented on. Pushing down hard on her pain, she stood like a queen, but she was screaming like a small child inside.

***

"Why'd you leave me?" Coral finally asked her parents.

"We were given no choice in the matter." Emerald shot a withering look at Sabella.

"Yes, it wasn't our choice." Morgan added a deep scowl.

"How's Ruby?" Emerald's face softened when she saw the heavy grief Sabella couldn't fully hide.

"She was in a car accident. Broke a foot and bruised her shoulder, but she's healing. At first they thought she wouldn't make it, but then she woke up."

"Yes, we saw." Sabella sighed, shaking her head. "She can heal herself, and you can heal her. Ruby trusted the wrong people, though, but then she didn't know there were wrong people, to begin with."

"We should have gotten them when they were on Oahu. Then this never would have happened." Emerald crossed her arms, and Coral saw a striking resemblance between her grandmother and her mom. Her throat tightened. She couldn't process a new family member right now.

Sabella raised her eyebrow. In a softer tone, she said, "Emerald, they were never in the water together. You know we watched for that, but it was more dangerous with the distance from our city. After the accident, well, we knew Ruby wouldn't be doing any swimming, and Coral was right here, so the time was right. Maui is in our backyard."

Emerald held Sabella's gaze as Coral spoke. "I don't understand."

"You see, Coral, they had found your mom's hidden gills at an experiment or, as they called it, a salty pool party. Your mom wasn't aware that she had them, but they knew. Those barbarians sent your mother to Maui intending to follow her when she swam. All I could do was rescue her and your dad. They certainly couldn't go back to get you after that. They kept your aunt, unable to find any gills on her, and watched you carefully. They knew from their intel that your change wouldn't come until you were this age. So confident that you'd lead them to us, they were willing to kill Ruby to get full control over you. I didn't want to go to war. Although I believe our magic is stronger than their weapons, I'd rather not test that theory. I apologize for the time you spent away from your parents, but I made sure to send those dreams to guide you. I hope someday you will fully understand."

Coral looked to her mom, not sure how to reply. Emerald shook her head. "I'm not even sure I understand, Mother. If that makes me unfit to rule, then so be it."

"There is nothing to understand. It is how it happened. This crown changes how you see the world. You'll see." Sabella gestured toward the pearls on top of her head and then crossed her arms. "Coral is here now."

Trying to take all this in, she pulled away from her parents and looked boldly at the older woman, who was apparently her grandmother.

"What about Aunt Ruby? You going to get her before they kill her too?" Coral crossed her arms, realized she was mimicking her grandmother, and quickly dropped them to her sides.

She heard a collective intake of breath from the group of people next to her. They were all staring at her in stunned silence. Maybe no one ever talked to their leader in such a way, but her aunt had been there for her. A slight smile crossed her grandmother's lips before she pursed them together and threw a commanding look at the group. "Coral, your aunt has become bait for them, so right now she's safe. That won't last, though."

"Will she be rescued then?"

"I'll do what has to be done."

"What has to be done?" Coral took a step back as her grandmother threw her chest out and knitted her eyebrows together over angry eyes. She wiped her sweaty palms on her swimsuit and quickly changed her tone. "This is overwhelming. I find out I can breathe underwater and heal people, my parents are alive, and I come from a ruling family in a gold city. Yet I was living with people who wanted to hurt me and tried to kill my aunt. We can't leave her behind. And the poor Penny family—what will those bad people do to them?"

And Ben? She felt a pain in her chest. Did they think she had drowned?

"I appreciate your loyalty. It will serve you well someday. I've been watching, and things aren't what they seem. I agree about Ruby, but that family you were so fond of, well, they're out for themselves, as all air people are." Sabella turned her gaze to Emerald.

Emerald nodded. She grabbed Coral's hand. "I know the Pennys have been like family, but Mr. Penny has been working with the people who want to hurt all of us. Mrs. Penny is ill, and they used that to control Mr. Penny. They promised him a cure when they found us, so he made sure you got here and your dreams continued. We think Ben may know too. He knows about your dreams and his mother, at least. You can take comfort in knowing Mrs. Penny and Beth had no part in it."

Coral felt tears run down her face. She looked at her dad, who had been unusually quiet.

"Your mom is right. Sorry, honey."

"I don't believe you! You're lying." Coral wiped away the offending tears. Mr. Penny? Impossible! And Ben—you couldn't fake what had happened between them, could you? Of course, her grandmother probably already knew about their relationship.

"I excuse the council. You have witnessed Coral's return." Sabella nodded to the group, who turned and left. "We do not lie, Coral. That father is a sad pawn who chose the wrong side. The true evil is the company your parents and aunt worked for. We won't go through all of this right now." Sabella turned to Emerald. "I'll give you a bit more time to reunite before she has to finish her job and then come back to us."

"No," Emerald pleaded. "Send me."

"And I'll go," Morgan added.

"You both need to stay here. They don't know you're alive, and I want it to stay that way. Coral's our best shot to retrieve Ruby."

Coral smiled. "Do you have a plan?"

"Yes, I do." Sabella grabbed Coral's hand and held her gaze. Suddenly it felt like an electrical shock coursed through her body. She pulled away, staring at her uninjured hand.

"What just happened?"

"Your healing power. I was positive you had it and helped you find it. All you have to do is pull it from your core. You now know what it feels like when it's working."

"I can't believe you're sending a child to fight our enemies." Morgan got close to Sabella, who didn't back away. "I hold you responsible, Sabella."

Sabella put a hand on his shoulder. "I just felt her power. She is much stronger than any of us will ever be."

"How?" Coral shook her head.

"It runs in our family, child, but it's been many generations since one as strong as you has come to us. When you return, you'll learn what you need to know, like about the Great War. Hundreds of our people left to start a life in the air without magic. They walked out of the water in the name of their leader and never came back. Living up there made some of them crazy, cruel, and greedy. You have so much to learn."

"The air people used to be us?"

"Some of them. Here we have order and magic. Please take the next few minutes to catch up with each other. Then, Coral, you'll go back with the dolphin. Ruby is being brought on a boat. I have faith that your power can help you extract Ruby from her greedy boyfriend, get her into the water, and bring her home." Sabella lapsed into awkward silence.

"I'll do it."

"I'd rather it was me." Emerald put her arm protectively around her daughter.

"I don't like any of this," her dad said. "I've spent every day thinking about you. How you were growing, if you were happy, if you missed us. I don't think I can survive losing you again."

"I agree. You aren't doing this alone. We're going with her, Mother, whether you like it or not."

"Yes, I was afraid of that. I'm sorry." Sabella raised her arm, and two tentacles shot up and grabbed Emerald's and Morgan's legs tightly.

"No!" Emerald screamed.

"She's a child! You can't let her do this alone." Morgan bent down and tried to pry the tentacle away, with no luck.

Sabella stood there like a stone statue.

"Release them! I said I'd go," Coral demanded. She even tried her healing touch on one tentacle, but nothing happened. She whirled and faced her grandmother.

"I'm sorry, Coral, no. All you need to do is get your aunt in the ocean. The sea creatures will do the rest. Don't lag, and get out of there if they find you. You come straight back to us. Then we'll sit down and have a long talk after I close the door to the world of those evil people."

"Her dreams show otherwise. You told me yourself. Not all air people are bad, Mother." Emerald laid her head on Morgan's shoulder.

"Just because one air person is the father of my granddaughter does not make me trust them. He has had to conform to us." Sabella turned to Coral. "See you soon. This shouldn't take long."

Coral stared at her parents, who were still tied up by an octopus.

"I love you, Coral." Emerald was watching Sabella walk away.

"Love you, sweetheart. You know you don't have to do this. Your grandmother can figure out another way." Morgan nodded toward Sabella.

"It makes sense that I go." Coral caressed her necklace.

"You're wearing the necklace we got you."

"It's all I had. Hold on to it until I get back."

"Stay," Morgan quietly urged.

Coral shook her head and took off her necklace, offering it to her mom, who held up her hands, refusing to take it. "No. You hang on to it. It's good luck. Trust your gut, and please be careful. You know if you refused to go, there would be another plan in place, right? These are some of the worst people you can imagine."

Coral put the necklace back on and studied the tentacles again. She knew her dad couldn't breathe underwater unless he had help, but her mom . . . She reached down one more time and focused on her hand and her core. The tentacle flew back into the water, and her mom was free.

Emerald smiled. "Free your dad. I don't have those powers."

"No. He'll be safer here. Sorry, Dad, but you can't breathe underwater, and I need Mom under the boat, just in case." Coral blew a kiss to her dad.

She knew he'd be mad, so she jumped into the water and grabbed the waiting dolphin.

"Wait!" Morgan yelled.

Her mom followed her.

"It'll be okay, Morgan. I think Mother expected this." Emerald climbed on a second waiting dolphin.

"Take care of her." Morgan had tears flowing freely down his face.

Coral frowned and glanced back at her grandmother, who had stopped walking. She was watching them with a small smile on her face, so her mom was right. The dolphins dove underwater. Soon the city was behind them as they exited the cave.

D. L. Finn

Chapter 20
A Rescue

Coral and her dolphin smoothly cut through the cool, salty water. She glanced over at her mom and smiled. This was what a mermaid would look like—long red hair streaming behind her like a watery cloak. Using one hand, her mom whisked off her soaked red dress to reveal a rainbow bathing suit. Wait, she planned this? So it hadn't been Coral's idea, after all. Coral's face reddened, and she frowned deeply at the deceit. Sighing heavily caused a barrage of air bubbles to tickle her neck. She slipped, and her dolphin did a quick maneuver that kept her upright as a turtle bumped hard against her leg with the edge of its shell.

Two words popped into her head: *Trust family.*

Did you just tell me to trust my family?

Yes. The turtle made direct eye contact.

Why haven't you spoken to me before?

No other words were pushed into her head, and the turtle swam away. Her grandmother did say they could communicate with the sea creatures. *Can't argue with a turtle.* She held back a giggle.

Coral's mom turned to her with a large grin and gave her a thumbs-up as the dolphins surfaced for the first time. Coral returned it. She saw the turtle several feet behind them. After the dolphins sucked in their air, they dove together like a synchronized swimming team. The water rushed past her face and clouded her vision. They slowed down, and her eyes cleared. There was a boat in the distance. Before they got to it, they veered off into a nearby cave. They surfaced for the dolphins to breathe again, and the turtle was no longer with them.

Coral pushed wet hair off her face. "Is that the boat?"

"That's what the dolphins say. We need to wait here until it's clear."

"Okay. I wish the dolphins would talk to me. I think the turtle did." Coral looked away.

"Oh? I didn't hear anything from the turtle. What did it say?"

"I'm not sure—something about family." Coral adjusted her bathing suit, which didn't need adjusting.

"Well, it takes some practice. You'll learn. It's one of the gifts our people have." Emerald had her eyes fixed on the cave entrance.

"Gifts?"

"Your healing abilities and use of energy are strong, like your grandmother said. We'll have plenty of time to figure it all out. Right now, I'm told, it's a good time to act. Let's figure out the best way to do this. I'm thinking you should be found washed ashore and passed out, with no memory of how you got there. That way they can't grill you on what happened. They'll take you straight to Ruby to make you talk, but we won't let them. They have no idea I'm here with you, and the sea creatures are on our side."

"You want them to capture me?"

"Well, yes, but we have whales and sharks on standby. That boat won't survive a direct attack, so don't worry."

"You can make them attack?"

"'Help us' is a better way of saying it." Emerald shrugged.

"Was this always the plan, for you to come with me?" Coral blurted out.

"I wasn't sure what to expect, but I planned for everything. As for your grandmother, who knows what's in her mind?"

Clarity washed over Coral. "She knew I'd free you."

Emerald laughed. "Yes. You remind me of her in some ways."

"Is that good or bad?"

Emerald reached out and patted her arm. "In her good ways. She does have a way of pushing my buttons, but I know she does it with love, no matter how mad she makes me. So all I can say to you is do the right thing and trust yourself. You have her strength and power."

"I hope I do. Will Dad be mad when we get back?"

Emerald scrunched up her face and then put two fingers close together. "Maybe a tiny bit, but he'll be so happy you're back with us it will soon be forgotten." She nodded at her dolphin. "It's time. You ready?"

"Yeah, I think I'm ready." Coral shifted on her dolphin.

"Don't forget to trust your instincts, and tap in to your core power when you need it. Think of it as using a wand, but it's inside you, and you don't need all those special words. Play your part, and when they take you to Ruby, heal her, and then get off that boat. Once you heal her, she will remember. We'll give you an hour and then strike. Unless they try to leave, then know the cavalry is right under you."

"I got it."

"And Coral, if it weren't Ruby on that boat, I wouldn't let you do this, but she is powerful—and she's my sister."

"We can't leave her behind." Coral straightened her spine.

"I know. I'll be right there if you need me, but I have a feeling you won't. Ready?"

"I'm ready." Coral felt less confident than she sounded.

The dolphins dove deep underwater, then split up. Coral's dolphin headed to shore while her mom went to the boat. She climbed off when they got close to shore and scanned the area. No one was around, so she walked to the edge of the water. Then she carefully arranged herself, from a dancer's perspective, to look like she'd washed ashore.

She closed her eyes and visualized herself as a dying swan on the water's edge, except the water kept hitting her face. Carefully opening one eye, she looked around, saw no one, and then crawled higher on the beach. The water was just touching her feet and legs now. Perfect.

The sun beat down on her, and she was starting to burn. She peeked. No one there, but she could see the boat off in the distance. It had come closer. Her dolphin leaped high out of the water. That had to be the signal that they were coming, or maybe it was trying to get the people's attention. The rumble of a boat engine coming in her direction was her answer.

"It's a girl!" a man shouted, and then there was a splash.

It was working. She kept still as someone sloshed their way out of the water. There was a chill as the sunlight was blocked. Someone was standing above her. She stayed limp as strong arms picked her up.

"She's breathing," an unfamiliar voice said.

"Let's get this lucky girl back to the boat." Coral almost opened her eyes when she recognized the voice. Aaron.

"We should put a life jacket on her."

"I doubt she'll drown, but yes, by all means, make her all safe." Aaron's sarcasm rolled through her, and she had to suppress a shiver. She kept still as cold hands secured a vest around her. "Good. Now follow me back to the boat. I'll hang on to her." His voice made her want to scream like the monster had just appeared in a movie.

"Yes, sir."

Coral kept up her act as she was dragged, face up, over the water. Aaron's flippers hit her back as he swam. That was intentional, but she refused to respond.

"Here, help me get her in." Aaron almost sounded sincere.

They laid her in the boat none too gently. The roar of the small engine filled the air as they headed to the bigger boat. Soon they slowed down.

"What should we do for her?"

"I'm positive she'll wake up soon. Get her on the deck, and take that jacket off. Then go back and keep up your survey of the surrounding water. I have a feeling this will get interesting."

"Yes, sir."

There was a grunt as she was lifted off the small boat onto the bigger one. The life preserver was removed. A splash and a shadow across her again. Aaron was watching her.

Time for the second act. "What? Where am I?" She put on her best confused face.

"Oh, there you are. You had us worried. Do you remember what happened?" Aaron's voice dripped with a sweetness that threatened to bring up her lunch.

"Happened?" She repeated and gave a little pause as if she was thinking. "Well, I was on a drive with the Pennys, and we stopped to eat—wait. Where are they?" She remained in her supine position on the deck. It wouldn't look good if she sat up too quickly after being passed out on a beach.

Aaron gave her that cruel shark smile. "They looked for you but finally gave up and headed back to the hotel when the authorities took over. Apparently you ate, swam, and simply went out too far and disappeared underwater. Fortunately I had rented this boat to take your aunt out for a relaxing day when she got released from the hospital. We were in the area when we got the call about your 'drowning'. We've been searching for you ever since. It's so lucky the captain spotted you lying on the beach a mere two miles from where you disappeared." He shook his head.

"You found her?" Aunt Ruby asked. A short, blond man with lots of tattoos was pushing her wheelchair on the deck. He was wearing a short wetsuit and looked like he spent a lot of time at the gym.

"Aunt Ruby!" Coral made a show of trying to get up.

"No, Coral. Stay down. You've been through a lot." Aaron smiled, but his eyes were narrowed. He looked at her like he was a great white and she was his prey. No one else was getting near her. "Yes, Ruby, she was lying right over there on the beach. Can you imagine everyone missing that?" Aaron kissed her aunt.

"Aaron had this all set up to help me heal. When we got the news, he was right here helping with the search. I can't believe you found her. Thank you so much!" Aunt Ruby tried to push her wheelchair closer, but the man held her in place.

"Anything for you. Please, Ruby, let the man take care of you. I promised the doctors you would rest. I'll keep your niece safe." He signaled for her to be taken away.

"You're the best, Aaron, and I can't believe she's alive, but I must hug her before I rest." Aunt Ruby gave Aaron her best smile. He had no idea, but Coral did.

"Well, let me help Coral over to you. After all, she's been through a lot, dragged out to sea and deposited on a beach. That's stuff you only read about in stories or movies, huh? Come on, Coral. Let's give your aunt a big hug and get her settled in. Then we'll let the coast guard and the Pennys know you're safe and well." Aaron pulled Coral up. His grip on her was tight, like he was worried she would bolt, but she wasn't leaving without her aunt. He had to know that was why she'd come back.

Coral pretended to get her balance back as he walked her over. She fell into Aunt Ruby's arms, being careful of her cast and her shoulder. Her aunt's eyes filled with tears as she gave her a one-armed hug. Coral focused on her core and sent a huge bolt of energy through her hands. Hopefully, it was enough.

"Oh." Aunt Ruby jerked and looked at Coral differently. Her face softened, and she smiled.

"Don't hurt her, Coral." Aaron put a hand on her shoulder.

Ruby shook her head. "She isn't hurting me, Aaron. It just felt good to hold her again after thinking we'd lost her. When I have a daughter someday, I hope she's exactly like you, Coral."

"Thank you."

Aaron tugged her away.

Ruby sat up straighter. "I feel so much better now that I know you're okay. They do say hugs heal, don't they, Aaron?"

"Hugs? Of course they do. I'll be hugging you all night, trying to heal you up. Don't worry about that, Ruby. Now you rest." Aaron's grip tightened on Coral.

Coral caught her aunt's eyes and looked at the water with a slight head bob that Aaron missed. Aunt Ruby nodded back. She understood.

"I'd like to lie down up here, if you don't mind, Aaron. I think the sun would do me some good."

"Well, okay. You rest, Ruby. I'll get Coral checked out. We'll be back soon." Aaron yanked Coral behind him. She scanned the deck. There were at least two other men in wetsuits who weren't part of the crew and were just there to watch her aunt.

"I need to use the restroom."

"Here." Aaron pushed her through a door.

Coral shut it but found no lock. She washed her face and studied the head. It was tiny, dirty, and had nothing lying around that would help her. She had no idea where he'd got this boat, but it wasn't as clean as she'd expect a rental to be. She took a deep breath and combed through her tangled hair with her fingers. The face in the mirror looking back at her wasn't the same face she'd seen that morning. It was more confident—and lacking the glasses that she no longer needed. Taking a slow, healing breath, she pushed through the door, ready to deal with her enemy and get her aunt into the water.

"Everything okay, Coral? I'll make sure your glasses are brought to you immediately." Aaron rushed over to help her sit down on the couch next to him.

"It's blurry, but I can make things out. I feel okay."

"Yes, you appear to be in good health after what you went through. Very odd, don't you think?" Aaron nodded to another man in a wetsuit, who picked up a tray of drinks and rushed it over to them. Aaron was used to being in command—that much was obvious.

"I can't remember."

"I'm sure your memory will return. Here, drink some water. Being in the ocean with all that salt can dehydrate anyone."

Coral took the sealed water bottle that was offered. She was thirsty, so she opened it and gulped down the cool liquid with the hope that it hadn't been tampered with. Aaron was handed a glass full of liquid amber that he began stirring as he watched her closely. How would she get back to her aunt and into the water with him on top of her like this?

"Hungry?" Aaron signaled, and a tray of sandwiches was brought to them.

"No, thank you."

A quick flick of Aaron's hand, and the man retreated from the room, leaving them painfully alone.

"So, let's figure out what happened to you. Maybe you could tell me about that golden city." Aaron smirked, making her shiver. Her mouth almost fell open, but she clamped it shut. "No response? No matter, just know I know many things: You aren't like the rest of us. Your parents abandoned you, and your aunt isn't like you or her sister. What else do I know? Plenty, but now it's your turn to share."

Coral contorted her face into a mask of what she hoped looked like confusion. "I don't know what you're talking about."

Unexpectedly, Aaron laughed. "You expect me to believe you were washed ashore two miles from where you were swimming without a scratch on you? Really, Coral?"

"I just know I'm here."

"Yes, you are here. I give you that. Did you expect to find your aunt here? I doubt that. I bet your plan was to be rescued and then see your aunt in the hotel. Later, you'd get her into the water, and off you two would go, back to your golden city. Sorry I ruined your plans, but then I've been waiting for this moment for a long time. My father learned about your city from that unfortunate water boy. It took a lot to get the information out of him, and sadly, he didn't make it. I'm sorry—I hope he wasn't related to you, Coral." He calmly sipped his drink, set it down, picked up a sandwich, and took a large bite out of it.

"Still don't know what you're talking about."

Aaron shifted so he was inches from her face, pushing his putrid breath at her. It smelled like a meal had gone bad in the fridge. "Let me enlighten you. My last name isn't Harvey. It's Dunning, as in the company your parents and aunt worked for. Dad taught me to keep a low profile. Our world requires what your people have—the ability to heal and to make gold out of any hard substance. Having both of those things could change my world. You understand how many people it would help, right? All you have to do is help me find this place so I can introduce myself."

Coral crossed her arms. "I have no idea what you're talking about."

Aaron sat up and finished his sandwich, never taking his eyes off her. "Unwilling to help? Selfish of you, but I think I can solve that issue. I have your aunt, and I'd hate for anything to happen to her." He leaned in close with a dangerous grin. "I think you might need to talk this out. I've brought your therapist here to help with that." He snapped his fingers. "Lilly."

Chapter 21
A Surprise Meeting

Lilly strutted out of a cabin next to the head wearing a sundress and large white hat. She looked like a tourist on vacation, not a therapist kidnapped to get her patient to give up information. She smiled brightly at Coral. "It is so good to see you. Aaron tells me you have information that would help him. I hope we can give it to him, don't you?"

"Lilly! Did they hurt you?"

"Hurt me? No, I'm not hurt. Are you?"

Coral felt a chill run through her body. Why was she acting so strangely?

"I'm not hurt. I just have no memory of what happened to me. And this man here seems to think I know about some golden city. I think he needs your help more than I do."

"Aaron? Need my help? I don't think so, Coral. You're confused, and I want to help you help yourself. I've always helped you, right? Let you quit therapy and get on with your life?" Lilly smiled so deeply and sincerely that Coral almost believed her.

"Yes, you were a big help, Lilly. I wish I could be of help now, but of course, I have no idea what you're talking about. Sorry." Coral shrugged.

"Of course you don't, after such a trauma." Lilly sat down on the other side of her and put a hand on her shoulder. "You must be so confused, waking up on this boat, not remembering how you got here."

"Yes."

"And to be found with not even a scratch is amazing. You're so lucky, Coral."

"Yes." Coral looked away, feeling claustrophobic. They had her boxed in, and she began to sweat.

"With all this luck you're having, maybe you could share some of it and help Aaron help the world. Then you and your aunt could go back home and forget everything that happened. How lucky would that be?" Lilly smiled at Aaron.

"Yes, Lilly is right. You're very lucky." Aaron smiled broadly at her therapist.

"I'm not feeling . . . lucky. I'd like to go back to my aunt now." Coral tried to stand up.

Aaron held her between him and Lilly. "Don't leave us so soon. My sister seems to like you, and I never get to spend time enjoying her company like this. You want my sister to be happy, don't you?"

"Your sister?"

"Yes, Lilly Harvey Dunning. She was the one who went to school and made Dad proud. You know, we never got along as kids, but look at us now. Dad would be pleased. Too bad he isn't here to see it. Sad, he died so early in life in a boating accident. Did you know that, Coral?" Aaron raised an eyebrow at his sister. "Right here on this very boat. He had a heart attack scuba diving. Broke our hearts, right, Lilly?"

Lilly nodded. "Yes, it did, but all the money made up for it. Imagine my surprise, Coral, when you came into my practice and told me about your dream right after my brother had filled me in about those water people our father had found! Why, it seemed too good to be true—and very *lucky*. All I had done up to that point was report back to my father on employee mental conditions as I worked my way up in the company. Made it easy to control them." Lilly winked at her brother before she continued in a firmer tone. "Coral, you must understand you won't be lucky enough to escape us."

"I don't believe in luck."

Lilly patted her arm. "You should. Keep your aunt safe—tell my brother what he needs to know, and everyone will leave happy. Tell me what you're thinking, Coral."

"I think you already tried to kill my aunt."

Aaron shrugged. "I won't lie to you, Coral, because I like you. I admit we believed she wasn't important, but we were wrong. She'll be very useful to us now, if she gets you to point the boat in the right direction. It's that simple—you can both walk away from this."

140

Coral shook her head. "You tried to kill her, and now you'll let her walk away. Very confusing messaging, and although I wish I could help you, I know nothing about a silver city."

Lilly smiled. "*I* didn't try to kill anyone, Coral. I'm just here to help you. I'm not worried about letting you go because who would believe a crazy story about an underwater city? How does that make you feel?"

"I feel nothing right now."

Aaron jumped in. "I'm positive those water people will want to talk with us about the *golden* city. Yes, I caught you trying to throw me off—good one, Coral. We have a wonderful deal waiting for them and us. And think about it. There are so many people you care for, like that sweet boy who has such a huge crush on you, and his sister."

"You're threatening the Penny family too?" Coral jumped up before Aaron could stop her.

Lilly was next to her in a flash. "I'll give you some space, and then we can talk about your feelings, Coral. I want to make sure you're okay with all of this—that is, after you do what we want." She giggled as she left the cabin.

Aaron was still next to her. She had to get back to her aunt and get out of there. They were both completely crazy. He put his arm around her. Her stomach protested, and she threw up. She wiped her mouth.

"Oh, dear. I'll have to get someone to clean that up. Well, you see, you can't win. All you can do is save your aunt." Aaron paused, but she remained silent, so he continued. "You notice I didn't even ask if you saw your parents because it would be unlikely they'd let you leave them again—unless you aren't as important as I thought. Your first reaction told me you'd seen the city."

"Don't know what you're talking about, Aaron."

"Of course, maybe your parents aren't alive, but your aunt is—for now. The woman who has taken care of you for the last eight years. Don't you want her to keep living? So why protect a city of people you don't know when you can save your wonderful aunt, who has done everything for you? What will it be?"

Coral remained silent.

Aaron sighed. "So stubborn. How about this information? Mr. Penny has been working for me. Wanted to save Sarah—how sweet. But of course that won't happen if you don't help me. Do you want to kill Mrs. Penny?"

"I don't believe you."

"But you weren't surprised. Good to know." He grasped her arm painfully and started to pull her out of the cabin.

"Hey!" Coral protested, wishing he couldn't read her face so well, but she still had one thing he didn't know about— her mom.

"Hay is for horses, as my grandma used to say. Not very helpful right now, though. Let's see how your aunt is doing. Make sure her shoulder and leg aren't hurting. Watch what you say, or your aunt will pay dearly for it." Aaron's face brightened when he saw Ruby. "Did you get some rest?"

"Yes. A little. Who was that woman I saw? She looked familiar," Ruby said, looking at Coral, who nodded slightly.

"Oh, this is her boat. No one you know." Aaron squeezed Coral's arm hard and then released it as he swung his leg toward her aunt's injured foot.

"Nope. No one we know." Coral scanned the deck. She would play along for a bit.

"Are you okay, Coral?" Aunt Ruby asked.

"Yes, I'm fine. I was just thinking about how much fun we had shopping for this trip, getting this necklace and all. But now you're hurt, and I almost drowned. Not what we planned, right, Aunt Ruby?" Coral smiled, making Aaron frown.

"Not at all what we planned, Coral. But at least it's beautiful on this boat. We're with good friends, and we're safe, right?"

"Right," Coral agreed. She hoped her aunt understood what she was trying to say. "You know, Aaron. I think you're right, and we should go to that perfect place and relax."

"Coral, don't," Aunt Ruby warned.

"Oh, Ruby, she's doing it for you. She's a wonderful girl. You did a good job raising her."

"I agree, she is wonderful, but I don't want her to do anything she doesn't want to."

"Oh, Aunt Ruby, it'll be okay. Look at those dolphins over there."

"I can't see them. Can you help me, Aaron?"

"Help you? Oh, sure, I'll get your wheelchair by the railing so you can see."

"Thank you."

"First point us in the right direction, Coral." Coral pointed the opposite way of the city. "There, that wasn't so hard. For your sake, I hope we find what we want."

"My only thought is to keep my aunt safe, don't worry."

Aunt Ruby groaned when he ran her foot into the railing.

"Are you okay?"

"Yes, fine, just moved wrong. Help me stand up so I can see."

"I don't think you should stand."

"Oh, I'll be fine if you help me, Aaron. Please. I love dolphins."

Aaron sighed but helped her aunt up.

Off to the side, Coral could see Lilly watching them. She was smiling.

"Okay, Ruby. Here, you hang on tight," Aaron said as the boat started up. He signaled someone, who started to navigate the boat away from the shore.

"Oh!" Ruby exclaimed. "Could you get my glasses? I left them over there, Aaron. Then you two can have your talk. I'm so pleased you're getting to know each other. It's wonderful."

"All right. I'll be right back." Aaron added in a whisper, "You better be right, or her entire leg will be broken next."

"Now!" Ruby said and jumped. Coral followed behind. Her aunt's cast split from her foot and fell off her leg into the sea. *How did she have time to do that?* They hit the water and were immediately met by her mom and the dolphins. Ruby shrugged off her sling and climbed on the back of a dolphin while Coral and her mom did the same.

Two divers were already there, then two more. It was as if they had planned for this. The divers had a fishing net. Others had weapons trained on them. It seemed like their plan hadn't worked. The net had almost closed around them when several large sharks came out of nowhere. They attacked the divers furiously, and Coral had to look away. The net loosened, allowing Coral, her mom, and her aunt to escape.

They made it into a cave, where the dolphins surfaced to breathe. Two sharks followed them. They moved on to another cave until they had put some distance between them and the divers. Coral couldn't believe there hadn't been more of a fight. Maybe Aaron and his sister weren't as smart as they thought they were. Yet she still didn't feel safe.

They kept going from cave to cave without staying in one place for very long. Coral hoped one of the caves would take them to the golden city, but they kept moving. The next time they surfaced in a cave, they didn't take off right away. The sharks remained outside. She scanned the wet darkness. Her eyes adjusted enough to see the outline of her mom and aunt.

"I think we lost them," Emerald said.

"The sharks were a nice touch, sis." Ruby tugged her sundress down.

"I thought so. As prepared as they were to capture us, they didn't expect that." Emerald chuckled. "I'm glad you got that cast off."

"Me too. Aaron had put a tracker on it. He thought I didn't notice. That plan also backfired. I'm surprised he didn't put something on Coral too." Aunt Ruby looked over.

"Nothing," Coral confirmed. "All I did was drink a sealed bottle of water."

"I have to thank you both for coming to get me, but you shouldn't have risked it."

"I wasn't going to leave you behind." Coral's dolphin swam closer to them.

"Yes, you weren't going to be left behind again. It was worth any risk. And Ruby, thank you for taking care of Coral."

"She's been like my own. I wish we'd gone with you and hadn't been left to deal with the grief of losing you." Aunt Ruby wiped a tear away. There was an uncomfortable silence. It was eight years they wouldn't get back, but at least they had the future together.

The water gently washed against the cave walls, black rocks formed by molten lava when it cooled in the ocean. Coral could hear the rumble of a boat's engine near them.

Emerald finally broke the awkward silence. "We were given no choice in the matter. I was told we were all going to be extracted in a few months during our vacation, but Dunning Corporation threw a wrench in that plan. You must know that I would never have willingly left my child or sister behind." Emerald pushed her hair out of her face, and Ruby remained silent. "I had no idea I was being used to find our city on this trip, simply because I had no memory of it. Dunning planned every detail, including their pilot getting sick at the last moment. They knew Morgan would take over flying the small plane.

"As soon as we got near Maui, we suddenly had no gas. It should have been a simple water landing for him, but before he could start the descent, both wings exploded. We hit the water hard, and that's all I remember until

I was back home. I was told Morgan had been able to get me out of the plane as it sank, and that was when our people came to get me. Morgan refused to let me go, and all they could do was help him breathe as we made our escape, with a pod of whales adding to the confusion. Luckily I'd taken off the wristband they insisted we all start wearing at work. I think that had a tracker in it, but it caused a rash. That was luck, and Dad refused to wear his." Emerald smiled.

"Very lucky," Ruby repeated.

"I've heard that word a lot today, and I believe in it now," Coral added.

"Luck was with us all today, Coral—and a bit of determination. I wasn't going to let them take my daughter or sister from me again. Understand, this is the first time I've been allowed to leave the city since I returned."

"It was more important to get Coral back. You shouldn't have taken a chance with her," Aunt Ruby almost whispered.

"I know, Ruby, believe me, but if Coral was allowed to go back to get you, then it was safe. She's very powerful."

"I don't feel all that powerful, Mom," Coral said.

"You are." Her mom patted her arm and then continued. "Dunning tests showed you were in so-called remission, Ruby—completely human per their tests—with your gills gone. You were left alone because of Coral. They were waiting for her to change and knew she was at the right age for it. Yet it all backfired on them again, didn't it? Nice to see your gills are back."

"Yes, just needed to get back into our ocean, I suppose." Aunt Ruby stroked her gills with a sour look Coral was very familiar with. "We aren't safe yet. We still have to get back home."

"No, we aren't, but we're as safe as we can be until we can continue."

"That's true, sis. Thank you for healing me, Coral."

"I'm glad it's something I can do."

Aunt Ruby nodded. "I know we can't live in their world anymore, but there are some things I'll miss."

"I know it isn't all bad, but what is ruins it for the entire world." Emerald sighed. She reached out to her sister and grabbed her hand. Ruby almost looked like she was going to pull away, but she didn't.

145

D. L. Finn

Chapter 22
Sisters

Coral blinked away tears as she watched the sibling reunion. Aunt Ruby was majestic sitting on top of a dolphin, confident and beautiful—like her mom.

Ruby ran her fingers through her hair with a sad smile. "I remember when we went to the air world, sis. We were going to learn as much as we could to bridge our two worlds. Then they located us and brought us into the fold at Dunning Corp after we forgot who we were. We were just well-paid lab rats to them. While I was on the boat, I overheard a conversation about Jade and Dad. Is it true?"

Emerald frowned. "Yes, sorry, it is."

Ruby lowered her head. "I feel like my heart has been ripped out of my chest."

"It's hard for me too, even after eight years. I was going to tell you when we got back to the city, Ruby. It hit Mother hard. She's not the same anymore, more withdrawn. None of this went as planned, but we have each other now. We have to focus on that. I'm not sure the air people will ever be ready for us." Emerald sighed.

Ruby rubbed her face and rolled her shoulders as she adjusted herself on the dolphin. "There's a cruelty in this non-magical land, and we lost people dear to us. But we got Coral out of it."

"Yes, but not all air people are bad. Many are good and innocent."

Coral felt like she had a lump in her throat. She was going to miss Tara, Ben, Beth, and her old life. The silence grew heavy, so she turned to her mom. "Shouldn't we get back to the city?"

A look passed between her aunt and mom. Her mom nodded at her aunt, who replied, "As much as your mom and I want to get you to safety, Coral, we still have some unfinished business to handle before we leave this land forever."

Emerald smiled. "We communicate by thoughts. I'll teach you later. We can't let Mrs. Penny die. Even though her husband did something stupid, well, it would be hard to live with. She's like family to us, isn't she?"

Coral frowned. "I'm not sure I agree. I mean, after what Mr. Penny did to me, to us . . . " She put her hands on her hips.

"It would haunt all of us if we let Mrs. Penny die." Aunt Ruby's tone was firm. "Anything Mr. Penny did was because he had no choice. His only part was leading you to the ocean, and I have a feeling he hoped you'd get away and reunite with your parents. Put your hurt feelings aside, and focus on some good that we can leave in this world."

Coral shrugged and fidgeted on her dolphin, who jerked so quickly she almost fell off.

"Well said, Ruby." Emerald reached down and stroked the side of her dolphin. It turned to look at her and nodded. "Your dad and I were forced to be apart from you. We had no choice. Mr. Penny was forced into a similar position. I'm positive he did everything for you and Ruby that he could. He's that type of man and shouldn't carry the burden of your and Ruby's death for the rest of his life along with losing his wife. This will be our only chance to do some good before we leave and the door between the worlds is closed forever."

Coral felt butterflies in her stomach at the thought of seeing Ben again. She missed him and his family, but were they worthy of her mom and aunt's trust, especially Mr. Penny?

"Tap in to your core. The answer is there, Coral."

She frowned but followed her mom's instructions. A confident surge rushed through her. Yes, they were. She nodded.

"Sabella—I mean Grandma—was pretty insistent that we come right back, but I can see and feel your point."

They both smiled, and her mom winked.

"Good. I think we'll have the element of surprise on our side. They won't expect us to go back there again now that you've rescued your aunt. While they look for us in the ocean, we'll be on land. Do you see the wisdom in letting them think they lost us in the ocean? You were staying at the same hotel where we used to stay, Ruby?"

"Same one." Aunt Ruby squinted as she studied the cave entrance.

"Let's do this before our chance is taken away. The coast is clear. Ready?" Emerald gently nudged her dolphin.

"Ready," Aunt Ruby tucked her dress under her.

"Coral?"

"Let's do this."

Mom, daughter, and aunt, on their dolphins, dove once more into the deep blue ocean. They passed a pod of humpback whales and a school of shiny silver fish near some seaweed. A tiger shark accompanied them for a while and then veered off suddenly to the left. Straight ahead, there was splashing and legs. They were back in civilization. They moved away from all the people, and the dolphins came up for air. There was the area Beth, Ben, and Coral had snorkeled. It seemed like years ago. A tall, jagged rock wall with a fence at the top stood between them and the Pennys. The dolphins swam away as two generations started scaling the cliff.

"Be careful," Aunt Ruby warned with a slight smile.

"I am." Coral carefully placed her foot and pulled herself up. It seemed like it took forever, but she only slipped once. She was worried someone would see them and report them for trespassing. However, everyone's attention was on three dolphins jumping and spinning. They were putting on quite a show. Finally she and Aunt Ruby were at the top, where her mom was waiting for them. Coral followed her mom and aunt over the fence.

***

Ned smiled. He knew they'd return for the Pennys. His boss had ordered him back to the boat twenty minutes ago, but on a hunch, he'd ignored that order. And now here were Ruby, Coral, and the very much alive Emerald Dover, whom he recognized from his research, climbing over the fence and heading into the hotel.

Quietly he followed them. No time for backup. Besides, he wanted full credit for this. He was ready to follow them when they came back to the ocean. They'd be clueless, and he'd find that city. He wasn't even surprised that Ruby's foot and shoulder were completely healed, because those people could do that. His guess was they were going to cure Sarah Penny's cancer. His boss had been right to trust him with this information. He would finally get his happily ever after. He smiled.

**

Once they got off the elevator, they stopped talking. Coral's mom tapped gently on the door. Mr. Penny opened it and froze in shock.

"Robert." Emerald smiled gently.

"Emerald? Emie? Is that you?"

"Who is it, dear? Tell them we aren't up to company now."

"This isn't company."

He stepped back and let them in. His face was so white Coral thought he was going to pass out.

"Who—" Mrs. Penny's mouth hung open as Ben and Beth whirled around.

"Coral!" Ben ran to her and engulfed her in a hug. Coral melted into his arms. "You're okay! You didn't drown! Ruby, your foot and shoulder . . . and Mrs. Dover, you're alive! I thought . . . this . . . I—I have your glasses, Coral." He pointed to the dresser with tears in his eyes.

Coral shook her head. "Don't need them anymore, but thank you, Ben."

Ben frowned slightly. "What's going on? Dad?"

"Those people we were forced to help—I just knew you'd get away." Mr. Penny's face seemed to crumble as he looked into the hall and then locked the door.

"Oh, they found Coral, who wanted to be found. Then she found me, and we parted ways with our hosts." Ruby smiled. "She healed me completely."

"How are you alive, Emie? This can't be!" Mrs. Penny gasped. "This can't be real. I must have taken too many pills. Or I'm asleep. Yes, that's it."

"Sorry, honey, it's very real." Mr. Penny put his arm around her and spoke in a soft tone. "I'm ashamed of my part in it. I had to believe Coral could get back to her parents where she belonged, but I wondered too. That's what I've been hanging on to the whole time. But that accident, Ruby—well, I had no idea they would go so far. I'm sorry is all I can say, and I hope you will all forgive me someday."

Emerald smiled and nodded. Aunt Ruby rushed to Mrs. Penny's side and hugged her.

Beth stared at Coral in shock. "Mom? Can I get you something? Dad, is she okay? Why is she that color?" Her voice was high, verging on hysteria.

"Beth, sweetie, it's time you knew. Your mom has cancer. She'll be okay for now, but I was doing all of this to help find her a cure. When I couldn't go through with it, they threatened not only my wife but my children. Ben overheard it all when I was on the phone. He knew about Mom's illness and that I had to do something for the company to save her. He didn't know it involved you, Coral. Don't hold this against him. He wasn't helping them, trust me. If I could change what's happened, I would." Mr. Penny sank into a chair.

Coral relaxed more under Ben's shoulder. His dad had confirmed what Ben had told her. She smiled and studied Mrs. Penny. She was pale, and it didn't look like she had much time left. She was glad they'd come back and wanted this moment to go on forever. She pressed up against Ben, feeling happy and protected.

A sudden gush of words spilled out of Beth's mouth like she was throwing them up. "Sick? How sick? You mean dying sick? And where has Mrs. Dover been all this time? Where's Mr. Dover? What did you have to do? Why did Coral disappear under the water? Will someone please tell me what's going on?" Aunt Ruby stood and put her arm around her.

"Please sit down next to me, Beth." Mrs. Penny patted the bed. "Let them explain."

"I need you all to remain open minded." Emerald held up her hand.

An awkward silence filled the room. Mr. Penny began studying the carpet pattern. Beth's and Mrs. Penny's eyes were glued on her mom. Ben kept trying to catch Coral's eye, but she couldn't look at him. Saying goodbye would be the hardest thing she'd ever done. Part of her wished there was a reason to be mad at him.

D. L. Finn

Chapter 23
A Decision

"Go ahead, sis." Ruby sat on the other side of Mrs. Penny. Emerald took a deep breath and let it out loudly. "Our time here is very limited. Dunning Corporation wants to find our people to make a profit off our powers, which include alchemy."

"You're aliens?" Beth's voice was a high-pitched squeal, like a car skidding around a corner, her wide eyes the high beams.

"We aren't from Earth, but we used to live with some air people, which is what we call you. A long time ago, a devout faction rejected magic and our way of life and left us. They mixed in with the air people."

"We were once magical?"

"Some of you were, but living on Earth, you lose your abilities. After a few generations, we believe, they were completely gone. Morgan, who's still alive, hasn't gotten any gifts since living with us, but maybe he didn't descend from us either. We wanted to offer our gifts to benefit your world. That ended very badly for us." Emerald paused and wiped a single tear away before continuing to a silent room. "My sister and I lived here and had forgotten who we were, which happens when we're here too long. Then my mother rescued Morgan and me, but that meant we were separated from our daughter and my sister. And Robert, we do forgive you because your actions finally got Coral home."

Mr. Penny mouthed a thank you to Emerald, but the pain didn't leave his eyes.

"Before we go and cut all ties with your world, we needed to say goodbye and leave you with a gift. Coral, you know what you need to do."

Coral unwillingly left Ben's side and stood in front of Mrs. Penny. Pulling on her core, she laid her hands on Mrs. Penny's shoulders. The energy raced through her, but when it came to her hands, it fizzled out. She tried again and again.

Mrs. Penny looked up. "That felt like a carpet shock. What was that?"

"I'm trying to heal you, but it dissipates before it leaves me. What's happening?"

Emerald crossed the room and took Mrs. Penny's hand. "I'm sorry, Sarah, it's too advanced. This is something that would have to be done in our world, where magic can sustain it."

"That's okay. I've come to terms with it. Thank you for trying, though." Mrs. Penny wrapped her arms around her sobbing daughter.

Emerald signaled for Coral and Ruby to come to her. "We need to get back before we're discovered, so here are a few more details that will help you survive your enemies. First, know that Aaron is behind all of this. He is the CEO of Dunning Corporation, and Lilly, the therapist that Coral saw, is his sister. Together they've been looking for our city ever since their father got a hold of our brother and father and killed them. They learned more about us than we would have liked, except how to find us."

"Aaron is the CEO of Dunning? You're kidding me." Mr. Penny's brow furrowed.

"No, unfortunately, I'm not. I can offer you one hope. If you let us take Sarah with us, we should be able to cure her, but she'd have to live with us. Your family would be separated, and I know how that is. Please talk it over, and let us know what you think. If you agree, I'd like you to rent her a scuba tank—I know she's certified—and we'd take her with us." Emerald smiled at Coral sadly.

Mr. Penny looked up at Emerald in disbelief. "You'd still help us?"

"Yes."

"But I'd never see them again," said Mrs. Penny.

"No. Your healing would only hold in our realm. Sorry." Emerald looked at Aunt Ruby, who shook her head.

"I will not leave my family, no matter how much time I have left. I want to spend every second with them."

Mr. Penny's eyes filled with tears. "Please go. It will save your life. I can live with that knowing you're okay."

"Well, I can't." Mrs. Penny shook her head, patting Beth's pale hand.

154

"Mom, you should go with them." Ben's face reddened.

"Please, Mom. Maybe they'll let me go with you." Beth looked at Coral.

"I'd consider that," Emerald replied. "But we don't have much time. You need to rent the tanks."

"The rest of my family goes, or I will not go. It's that simple." Mrs. Penny winced. She opened her drawer, grabbed a handful of pills, and washed them down with some old coffee.

"I'm not sure I can convince our queen to take your whole family, especially Robert and Ben. There'd be concern about their loyalty and our world's safety. Although I don't hold it against you, it did happen. But with Sarah and Beth, there are no concerns." Emerald's tone matched Sabella's.

Mr. Penny put his head in his hands and began to sob. It scared Coral. He was always so brave.

Ben put an arm around him and looked sadly at Coral. "I'm sorry I kept things from you about my mom and a cure, but I had no idea what the price was to get it. You know how I feel about you. Could my father and I be put in prison until the queen can decide if she can trust us or not? Then we could be together in the same world, and my mother doesn't have to die." He sat down next to his father.

All eyes were on Coral, so she followed her heart and spoke her mind. "Ben, take your dad and rent four tanks. I trust you not to betray us." She had her grandmother's tone too. *Must run in the family.* She held her breath, waiting for her mom to argue.

Emerald smiled and nodded. "I can extend the welcome to all of you since my daughter believes in you enough to speak for you. As the queen-in-training, I invite you to live in our kingdom. If you remain loyal, you will remain free."

"Thank you." Mr. Penny wiped his eyes and firmed his shoulders.

"Let's get ready," said Mrs. Penny.

Ruby winked at Coral and helped Mrs. Penny up. Coral got the extra key for her room from Mrs. Penny. She neatly stacked her stuff in the corner, then added items to a waterproof bag—the camera, cell phone, the Christmas gifts for her aunt, and her mother's book—and stuffed them into the backpack. Maybe there was a way to look at the pictures where they were going. She wished she could let Tara know she was okay, but that wasn't safe. She yanked on the yellow shirt Tara had gotten her for

Christmas over her suit and, with a lump in her throat, closed the door to her old life for good.

She entered a room of busy.

"I don't know what we should take?" Beth had an armful of clothes.

Emerald smiled. "Everything you need will be provided."

"But our stuff . . . "

Mrs. Penny hugged her. "We're taking the most important stuff—us."

Ruby took the clothes from Beth and set them on the bed. "Take only what's truly important and that will fit into Coral's backpack. Think small."

"I should take Ben's extra glasses, my new dress—"

Coral interrupted. "Here, let me help you."

"So my suit, dress, and his glasses?"

"I took my camera to show my dad the pictures—if it will work. At least it has a full battery. I have almost two years on the card to share, and the camera is waterproof. I brought my cell phone for the other pictures, if it survives the trip, along with my mom's last book. I added a couple of things I got for Christmas. You should take your new jewelry, your camera, and that dress you love. It will remind us of this world."

"Good idea."

"That will be enough, Beth. We'll make new memories and acquire new things." Mrs. Penny had changed into her suit and cover-up.

The two girls packed up all the family's vacation stuff and set it by the door. Ruby and Emerald went back to their room so Ruby could get her bathing suit and take off her soaking dress.

Soon everyone was back together. Aunt Ruby had on her new earrings, but no glasses, just like Coral. Mr. Penny had put all the rented gear on the beds. Ben added his e-reader, cell phone, and ukulele wrapped tightly in plastic to Coral's backpack. Ruby zipped up her pack, which contained all the items the adults wanted to bring. They were ready to go.

Coral grabbed a leftover ham sandwich on the way out. She had never tasted anything better.

Beth was the last one out. She hesitated and then, with a loud sigh, shut the door.

They hurried through the hotel to the beach like they were in a spy movie, checking behind them and around each corner. Mr. Penny refreshed his family's memory on diving protocol.

"Lucky we all got certified, isn't it, Dad?" Beth adjusted her mask.

"It was a wonderful birthday gift for me." Mr. Penny scanned the beach as his family entered the ocean.

Beth and Ben took one last look. Soon they were swimming out to where everyone was snorkeling. The dolphins started jumping again, catching the swimmer's attention. Seven dolphins disengaged from the show and met them where there were six turtles but no people.

"Ready?" Emerald asked.

Mr. Penny held up his hand as he made one more check on his family perched on dolphins. He nodded to Emerald. They dove into the water, leaving their world behind.

***

Ned sat on an electric underwater swimmer in his wetsuit and top-of-the-line diving equipment. Now he'd find their golden city. They went fast and deep, and so did he. He was an experienced diver and had trained many hours on the swimmer.

Ruby, Coral, and Emerald reminded him of mermaids, riding dolphins with their hair flowing behind them. The others looked clunky with their equipment. He wanted to be like the women and breathe in both air and water. As they headed into the open sea, he saw Emerald turn around. He veered off to the right and gave them some distance without losing them, but he met up with a big tiger shark. He made a jarring left to lose it, but another shark was waiting. He was at full speed, but it wasn't enough. The shoreline was too far away. A third shark closed in on him, and sadness flowed through him. He'd never see the city, feel its magic, or get his reward. The sharks attacked, and then he lost consciousness.

***

Emerald was aware that someone was following them. Protecting her family and friends was her priority, and she felt no remorse in calling on the sharks to stop this person. They were usually gentle creatures unless they were feeding. They would mistake a human for food in those rare instances, but they didn't hunt humans like in the air people's movies. And they would keep her family and friends safe if she asked. The dolphins surfaced for air and dove only a couple of feet below the surface to keep the Pennys safe.

Emerald glanced over at her daughter. Pride soared through her. Her daughter had stood up for what was right by keeping the Pennys together. She'd be a great leader someday, strong and kindhearted, which would lead to wise decisions. Although Emerald wasn't a fan of using her mother's tactics to find these things out, Coral had passed with flying colors. Hopefully, her mother would see it the same way.

It was a time of new beginnings, and her daughter was strong enough to lead the way. The only thing that concerned Emerald was whether Coral would embrace the rest of her family, but soon her daughter would learn everything. Coral glanced over at her mom and smiled. Emerald smiled back.

***

The dolphins took the group under a large white boat—Aaron's boat. Coral could sense that only the captain, Aaron, and Lilly were on board, but the divers weren't far away. They were so close to the golden city, and they had no idea.

In his wetsuit, tank, and face mask, Ben reminded her of an aquatic superhero. What was going to happen between them in the new world? Would he stay interested in her as she changed and grew? Would it change how she felt about him? They had some things to work out, but she was glad they were going to get that chance.

The dolphins suddenly shifted course, startling Coral, who hung on tightly. She expected them to surface soon, but instead of going up, they went down, streaking toward a jagged rock wall like they were going to crash into it. Coral threw a glance at her mom, who appeared calm. Then an entrance appeared. It was a clever camouflage, but how long before Aaron and Lilly saw past it?

The group quickly surfaced as the dolphins sucked in air. The Pennys pulled off their masks. Ben's eyes were huge. Even though his glasses were in her backpack, his mouth fell open in pure awe. That was how she felt about this place too. The council was back on the dock, along with her grandmother and dad—who wasn't held down by an octopus anymore.

He had a huge grin on his face. "Welcome!"

A part of her wondered what the world they'd left behind would think about their disappearance. She didn't care as long as no one ever found them. She pulled herself out of the water and ran to her dad.

Chapter 24
Off the Radar

The white boat was still anchored where Ruby and Coral had fled. The divers were fed a false scenario and sent out to find Ruby Hyde, the escaped leader of a terrorist cell that had threatened Dunning Corporation and their country. It was no surprise to Aaron that his sister's plan came up short again when a frenzy of tiger sharks, hammerheads, and great whites swarmed the divers. No one had been seriously injured, and Lilly pushed them all back out to search until their tanks were empty. All they found were the pesky humpback whales who migrated to the islands every year. No entrance to Ruby Hyde's terrorist hideout was located.

Aaron asserted his authority and sent all the divers except two back to their compound to rest. The two he kept were men who had earned his trust. The others would meet with unfortunate accidents when they were done. Like his father, he knew how to clean up a situation.

His biggest situation right now was Lilly.

She paced and threw out orders to his two remaining men. "Find new tanks and get back out there. Check the area where that stupid whale is, birthing or not. Shoot it if you have to. Go into every cave and crevice. Look under things. Find them." The men quickly obeyed.

Aaron shook his head, confident he'd be the one to get what his family desired: absolute power. He frowned and rubbed his temples, letting his sister know he was displeased, but she didn't glance his way. That meant Lilly was formulating an expensive Plan B. He had an answer in motion to resolve this problem. He just had to play along a little bit longer.

159

Lilly startled him out of his guilty thoughts. "They have to be close by. It's the only thing that makes sense. At least we know they control sharks, and soon we'll be able to do that—once we find the city." She shook her short brown hair, and it settled into a messy style that suited her.

He faked a bored yawn. "Too bad we can't track Ruby." A shudder ran through him as he thought about having to flatter that woman. It had been like spending time watching mud dry in the sun. Dull didn't even begin to describe her.

"You should have put a tracker on Coral and given that woman some jewelry with one in it. I can't think of everything, Aaron." Lilly rolled her eyes.

"The cast was a good idea."

She shook her head with a smirk. "Sure, if she was going to swim with it on. I know they can't be far. I have every intention of locating that city and finishing what Dad started. We aren't leaving here until we find it." She put her hands on her hips and narrowed her eyes. "And I don't want to hear about the cost." She turned dramatically and walked away like she was on a runway. Now she would formulate a new plan to spend all their money. All *his* money.

Not this time.

He smiled and waved to Lilly like they were best friends on a wonderful vacation. She reciprocated. He headed to the cabin for privacy to make his call. With the board on his side, Lilly's shares would go to him. Perhaps it wasn't completely legal, but there was nothing she could do about it after the fact. He'd provide her with a generous trust, as their father should have done in the first place.

"Randall, good to hear your voice," Aaron began. "I hope all is in order?"

"Yes."

It would be final in three days.

***

Ned crawled onto some jagged black rocks. He was bleeding, but none of his wounds were deep. He didn't understand why the sharks hadn't killed him. Maybe it was simple luck, but he hadn't been lucky when he lost his quarry. The only thing that had worked in his favor was that Ruby hadn't seen him up close. She'd recognize him from the mailroom at Dunning Corporation without any disguise, and that wasn't allowed. He would have had to take care of her like that other operative, Kini.

This job—watching Ms. Hyde and her niece—had been part of his life for a while now. He'd even tried to date Ruby, as requested. He was way out of her league, but the stuck-up spinster hadn't even shown an interest in him. But he always got near enough to obtain the samples his boss required. He did his job well, just like in the navy.

All those years he'd served his country—until his country didn't want him. He was only doing what his commander wanted him to do, even if he didn't say so. No matter—he'd quickly found Dunning Corporation and spent the last ten years working hard for the father and now the kids. The strength of the father was in only one of his children. Ned was proud of that one boss—very proud indeed. He made the call he dreaded.

"Why aren't you at the boat yet?" the familiar voice asked him.

"I've been searching. I just saw your message." He had no intention of admitting his last failure. His gut never failed him, even if the circumstances did. His superiors in the navy hadn't understood that about him.

"Come directly to the boat. I'm texting its location now. You have a loose end to tie up, and it's time to carry out the final act. Then our full focus will be on finding this city."

"Got it, boss."

Ned went back to his black Jeep and retrieved the aluminum boat that would take him to the white boat. The location came through as he deposited his dented electric underwater swimmer in the back. Soon he was being tossed around like a baseball during practice on the choppy waters. The old yacht and a small island came into view.

***

Sabella waited quietly nearby as everyone embraced. She wasn't pleased about the air people being here, but she wasn't surprised. Mr. Penny did not have her trust, and there were several options she needed to consider. The main goal was to protect her people from the air people's corruption, which meant finally closing the door to their world—hidden behind a hologram and a whale.

The crowd parted, and she smiled. The person that had been the brightest star in the last few years smiled back at her. Her heart was full as he turned his attention to the reunion.

***

"Mom, you're back!" the young boy called.

Coral caught her breath as the boy raced into her mom's arms.

161

Mom?

"Coral, Ruby, I'd like you to meet someone. This is our son, Dylan."

Coral's mouth flew open, and then she snapped it shut. He looked exactly like her—no, *their*—mom, with red hair and green eyes. He was grinning expectantly at Coral.

Stunned, Coral responded in a voice that sounded more like her Aunt Ruby's. "Hello, Dylan."

"Hi, Coral, Aunt Ruby."

Ruby pulled him into a hug. "Hi, Dylan."

"I thought you couldn't have any more kids," Coral blurted out, feeling Ben's eyes on her.

"We thought so too." Emerald chuckled.

Her dad winked at her. "Yes, it was a surprise, but a good one, right, Coral?"

"Yes, a great one." Coral studied her new brother in his aunt's embrace. He pulled away and faced Coral.

His grin was exactly like their dad's. He grabbed her hand. "Coral, would you like to see our house? There's a room waiting for you."

"Yes, I'd like to." Coral glanced at her parents for confirmation. Her grandmother was observing them. She wasn't very friendly, especially with Ruby, who she hadn't seen in years.

"Come on," Dylan tugged on Coral. Their mom nodded with a smile.

"Let your brother give you the tour," her dad said. "We'll catch up to you after we get the Pennys settled."

"Okay." Coral glanced at her grandmother, who was watching her aunt. *Did Sabella have tears in her eyes?* She didn't have time to think about it as Dylan pulled her through the parted crowd of people and down a ramp. It was hard to keep up with him. Breathless, she was surprised that he continued his silence as they stepped into the golden city on a smooth cobblestone road, cool on her bare feet.

The city was a mixture of many styles—most she couldn't name, except for Roman, Victorian, and modern, with a dash of mountain living that included a golden log house with a big front porch and a swing. It all blended in a way Coral could never have imagined, making it a grand and whimsical city. The plants looked like they belonged in a children's book. Bright blue, purple, red, yellow, pink, orange, and green, with some black leaves mingled in like someone had thrown paint on a landscape. Coral

162

would have to study it later—Dylan impatiently yanked her to the right. Being a big sister would take some getting used to.

"Hurry, Coral! I have a surprise for you."

Coral exhaled a laugh. "I can't wait, Dylan. And I'm very glad I have a little brother. I've always wanted one, you know."

"You did? Mom and Dad weren't sure you'd be happy about me."

"Well, they were wrong. I'm very happy."

People peered out the windows of the buildings towering over them and then quickly closed their drapes when they saw her looking. "Why are they hiding?"

"They're staying inside so you won't get overwhelmed by all of us. Grandma insisted. We are many, and everyone would want to hug you, Coral, especially since you're our leader's eldest grandchild. Dad told me that you, Mom, and Aunt Ruby are heroes."

"Who, me?" Coral laughed. "I just got my—no, *our*—aunt off a boat and into the water. Mom did the rest. Then Mom and Aunt Ruby wanted to save Mrs. Penny. I just went along to help."

"Dad usually isn't wrong—unless Mom says so. So you must be a hero too," Dylan solemnly informed her.

Coral giggled. Her parents hadn't changed a bit. "That's true, Dylan, but maybe Mom will tell him he's wrong this time."

"We'll see." He didn't look convinced.

All the signs were written in English. Good—no need to learn a whole new language. They rushed past a library, which would make Ben very happy, a school, a food market, clothing stores, a hardware store, restaurants, a saloon, and other places that weren't marked. The street they were passing through was set up like an old western town—like Scuttle Valley—except it was made of gold. She seriously doubted there were any slot machines in this place. People were always trying to win in Scuttle Valley, and here it looked like they lived in the winnings.

Around the corner was Scuttle Wedding Services, which appeared to be both for wedding planning and a place to hold the event. How weird was it that she came from a town that had the same name? She would have a lot of questions for her parents when they got the time.

D. L. Finn

Chapter 25
A New Family

There were no cars or bikes on the streets. But on the waterways that wove through the city, there was an abundance of boats in every size and color. It reminded her of a place she'd always dreamed of seeing—Venice, Italy.

Something blue flew over them, casting a long shadow.

"Tillie!" Dylan called.

"Tillie?"

Dylan nodded and clapped his hands. "Yes, she's my dragon."

"A dragon? They're real?"

"Yes, very real. Just look."

"There she is! Does Tillie stay in your room?"

Dylan shook his head and kicked a loose pebble with the tip of his worn brown shoe. "No. I've tried. She goes back to the other dragons every night. Mom says your world only has stories of dragons. Her theory is that those who left here still have buried memories. Are the air people different than us, Coral?"

"Not that I can tell. Only they can't breathe underwater like us."

"Dad mentioned that, but I wondered—guess he was right." Dylan never took his eyes off his dragon.

"He is."

He ran ahead of her down a street with gold houses that looked like the painted ladies of San Francisco—except they weren't painted, just different tones of gold with silver and copper mixed in. The houses had yards, plants, and windows made of glass, like where she'd grown up. But this residential street was unbelievably beautiful. Was she going to live in this magical place? Off to the left, something furry ran by.

Dylan stopped and pointed. "That's Lane. He likes to chase Tillie and make her mad. They're both my beings, but neither will come to me. It makes me annoyed sometimes, but that's okay cause I know they love me anyway." He smiled. "Lane! See how he ignores me?"

Coral laughed, wishing she'd grown up with Dylan. She tried calling the furry creature. "Lane?" A small, dark brown animal came slowly out of its hiding place and stared at her before it blinked and retreated into the bush. It had a wild look, its fur going in every direction. "Is that a cat?"

"That's Dad's term. We call it a chat, which I know Dad says is French for 'cat,' but we don't speak French here. We have a universal language, which I'm sure you can read?"

"Well, I can read everything I've seen so far."

"It's something you're born with. Poor Dad had to learn it from scratch, and sometimes I have to help him. You'll see. But we were talking about Lane. Some chats can change their shape, making themselves bigger or smaller. All chats can swim, and they can fly, but only once a month during the new moons. I think that's why Tillie makes Lane so mad. At least they can swim together."

"We don't have animals like that where I come from."

Dylan looked horrified. "You don't have animals? Really? Dad never said that!"

Coral suppressed a grin. "We have animals, just not ones that fly once a month or change size. Our cats pretty much sleep all day and play or hunt at night. Our birds fly and have nests where they lay eggs. Does Tillie blow fire?"

"Of course. All dragons do. Doesn't matter, though, because everything is gold and our plants are fireproof, including the wood. Dad told me you get fires in the air world that they can't control in the forests."

"We do, from lightning, dry conditions, winds—and people start fires too. It's a good thing none of the birds breathe fire, because our houses would burn down." Coral adjusted her swimsuit.

"You're kidding me, right?" Dylan stopped on the golden walkway. "You build your houses out of stuff that burns?"

"Yes, and not only houses, but towns, and you already knew about forests."

"How strange. It's a good thing you never got hurt there. I'm glad I live here." Dylan sat down on the steps of the prettiest house Coral had ever seen. A small version of an old European castle—complete with turrets—it looked like it belonged in a fairy tale. It made the houses next to it look plain—and they weren't plain.

Dylan patted the step next to him. "I should tell you more things about us. Well, Dad thought I should, because he said the way we live is going to be different for you."

She sat next to her brother. "Yes, I think I could use some advice for living in a gold city."

"I know you saw the name of this city is Scuttle. Dad told me you lived in a place called Scuttle Valley. He thought that was strange—no, the word he used was 'weird.' Do you think that's weird, Coral?"

"Mom used to love the name of our town. Said it was the best name ever, but I never understood. Now I do. Yes, I would agree—it is weird and wonderful at the same time." She leaned against the warm gold rail on the stairs. She wondered why the metal wasn't cold to the touch since the sky was gray and cloudy.

"The kingdom—I mean, where you came from—it was a place called the United States?"

"Right, but there were other places, much like kingdoms. They all formed together in what we call Earth. Are we still a part of Earth?" Coral stretched her legs out and dug her toes into the soft green grass.

"Earth has one moon. Here we have two moons. This is a better version of Earth. If I'm confusing you, let me know. I'm smart, and not everyone follows what I say."

Coral nodded. "So this is like another dimension, and the cave I came through connects us, right?"

"That's what Mom and Dad call it, but Grandma calls it a door. This place we live in is called Mearth, not Earth. Which literally means 'Earth with magic.' How did you live without magic?"

"Very easily, not knowing it existed outside of stories. We do have people who pretend to have magic, called magicians. They only trick people, though. It isn't real. Maybe you can answer this for me. I know I can heal—is that considered magic here in Scuttle?" Coral was suddenly breathless.

Dylan pulled his head back. "Fake magic? Weird. Magic is just a part of who we are. Everyone has their magic or gifts. We're all able to communicate with all creatures if we learn their language, unless you were already born with that gift. We hoped Dad would get some magic living here, but so far he hasn't."

"Too bad."

Dylan shrugged. "It is. For us it's easier to communicate with animals in water than land animals. Mom can communicate with all creatures, including Lane. But no one can communicate with the dragons in our kingdom except Grandma and me. It runs in our family. Not everyone in our family has it."

"So you talk to dragons?" Coral was trying to absorb everything her little brother was telling her. It was all so unbelievable.

"I do, and Grandma has been teaching me how to train and control them. You know they can be kind of, well, Grandma calls it obstinate—like a bad kid. Tillie is the only one who comes to the city. Grandma's dragon hasn't been here in years. They live outside the city in the pink trees over the cliffs. I want to take you there soon—you'll like it. When Tillie gets big, I'll be able to ride her. Maybe you're like me and will get your own dragon. Montrose, Grandma's dragon, isn't as friendly as Tillie. Grandma's barely ridden him since, well, since she lost Grandpa and Uncle Jade." Dylan watched his dragon circle over them. Coral could tell it was eyeing Lane.

She leaned forward and placed her elbows on her legs, resting her chin on her hands. "That's sad. Maybe she will now that we're all together, although I can't picture Grandma on a dragon."

"Maybe. I can picture her on one because she taught me everything I know."

"I'm glad. Well, I'm a healer, and you control dragons. What else can we do?"

Dylan pushed back his unruly red hair and wiped his nose with the back of his hand like any typical boy. "What's normal for me might not be for you, Mom warned me. You're a leader like Mom, so you should be able to see people's dreams, like Grandma, at some point. Someday you'll monitor things outside our kingdom."

"I can't do that now."

Dylan shook his head. "No, not now. Let me see what else I can tell you. Oh, there are four kingdoms on Mearth where people live along with their

168

beings. They all have their own type of magic. Here we have the dragons, and there are unicorns in Lamer Kingdom. Those unicorns are very ill tempered, mainly because they don't like dragons. The leprechauns in Lockness Land and the fairies get into all kinds of trouble, like on last Mearth Day. I'll show you our pictures. And the leprechauns aren't little, like Dad thinks they should be, nor do they have a pot of gold. Then there are what Dad calls Bigfoots, or the yetis—they mainly collect plants and heal all growing things. They live in Melidrome City and are known to go to other worlds to collect samples. They have plants from all around the universe."

"Whoa! That's a lot to take in, Dylan. Leprechauns, fairies, Bigfoot, and unicorns? These are things from our fairy tales."

"Not fairy tales here, but it's the same theory for them as for the dragons. Dad was surprised how intelligent dragons are when he met them. They had all kinds of questions for him about Earth. The Lamers are the closest to us, and some of their land is dry like a desert. The people who live there travel on flying carpets. So don't be surprised to see one gliding above you."

"So the unicorns, dragons, Bigfoot, leprechauns, and fairies are intelligent like the people?"

Dylan puffed up his chest and nodded to Tillie, who flew off. "They are. The fairies—well, they just get into a lot of mischief. We have contact with other worlds, and with better success than Earth. My favorite place is a planet that has elves, where it's always winter. It's called the North Pole. Santa runs that and visits us once or twice a year. Not on a special day, though, like he's confined to in other places, but he always brings me a gift when he comes. You ever seen him?"

"So you're telling me Santa exists?"

"Yes, of course he does. I guess that means you haven't met him yet. You will here. His world isn't too far away. And yes, we celebrate Christmas. Mom explained it's different here, though. We put lights and decorations everywhere the night before. It's a big party, and we do lots of nice things for everyone—kind of like giving gifts, but not. We become Santa, but with deeds, not things. We have a big dinner. Dad misses pumpkin pie and turkey, but we have no pumpkins here, nor do we eat animals. We do have good desserts."

"Wow. Very cool." Coral smiled.

Dylan nodded and then frowned. "Are you cold?"

169

D. L. Finn

Coral hid her mouth under her hand. "No, not at all. The word 'cool' means 'great.'"

"Oh, right, a slang word. I've heard that one before, I think."

"Right."

Dylan moved closer and looked up into her eyes. "Are you happy you're here?"

"Of course I am. I'll miss my friends, especially my best friend, Tara, but I missed Mom and Dad more. Plus, I have a brother. So very happy."

"Good. You'll make lots of new friends here."

"I hope so. This is all so different for me. It'll take some getting used to."

"You'll learn as Dad did. And I'll help you a lot. For instance, we don't have wars or fights here, not since the Great War. We share and work together, yet we have leaders who do what's best for the group, like Grandma. Like in your place, we vote on new rules and heads of areas once a year, under Grandma. Everyone has a say. Then we follow them until the next year and vote them in or out again. Grandma meets with the other leaders from the four realms twice a year. They make rules and are the contacts for the others from distant places." Dylan spoke like he was giving a speech in class.

"Sounds reasonable to me."

"It is. Having Grandma as our queen brings consistency. And we have a shield to protect us that we have never had to use before—well, until now with Earth, which we will be doing soon. But everyone else can still visit, including Santa. He feels spreading goodwill to Earth and other planets will make a difference. Santa has a theory that magic is coming to Earth, but Grandma disagrees." He grabbed her hand. "I'm talking too much."

"Oh, no, you aren't. There's so much I want to know, and you're giving me lots of good information." Coral stood up and held her free hand out to Lane, who started toward her slowly.

"I'll try to tell you as much as I know if you promise to tell me about Earth. I don't think Mom or Dad tells me the whole truth. When you're as smart as me, you know when people are telling the truth or not. Come here, Lane."

Lane looked at Dylan, sat down, and started cleaning himself.

Just like a cat.

"It's a deal. We'll teach each other."

Dylan started swinging her hand and didn't seem to want to let go. Neither did she. "Look. Lane's teasing Tillie again."

Tillie had come back and was circling them. Then she flew off. Lane looked up, shook his tail, and calmly strolled away as though Coral, Dylan, and Tillie didn't exist.

Coral giggled. "Do you think the Pennys will be okay here without magic? How's Dad handling it?"

"Dad does fine. Mom showed him all he needed to know. Although Tillie and Lane don't like him, everyone else respects him. I think they'll do the same with the Pennys. They'll watch and see what our family does. Oh, you'll like school here. I started last year, but I had to be moved up because of my intelligence."

"I can tell you're very intelligent. I'm in what we call high school, and I'm in my normal grade. I was going to college after, which isn't required but helps if you want a certain type of job."

"I'm sure they'll catch you up to your age quickly. It's a good idea to learn more."

"I don't mind learning. Oh, does anyone drive on land, like in a car?"

"We don't have them. We do use boats on the water to get around, but mostly we walk. You're old enough to drive a boat here. Then we fly to further places." He released her hand.

She felt tempted to mess up the hair on the top of his head but had a feeling he wouldn't understand why she was doing it. "Is there dancing and music here?"

"It's not called those things, but I understand what you're asking. Mom and Dad explained these things to me before you came so I'd know about dance. Here dancing is 'flowing like water.' It's very popular, and I'm sure everyone will want to learn how you do it. As for music, it accompanies our singing. It's a gift to know how to do that. Do you do that?"

"I don't play music or sing, but Ben—one of the Pennys—plays the guitar, like Dad did, or does?" Coral blushed.

Dylan started moving from one foot to another. "Dad does. We all sing, and Dad plays his guitar here. He's been teaching others to play. He also teaches soccer, and I participate. Do you play?"

"I used to, and Dad used to coach my team, but I don't anymore. I just dance, but I look forward to watching you play."

D. L. Finn

"I'm pretty good at it, but we don't start again for a couple of months. Oh, it's usually cold here this time of year. We've had a warm spell, but you wait—you'll need a coat soon. Mom said you would want to know that. You aren't thirsty right now, are you?"

"Thirsty? No, why?"

"Well, before the change, you're thirsty all the time. After you change, you aren't as much. I wasn't sure if you were completely done. I'm thirsty all the time." Dylan's face transformed solemnly as he clamped his mouth shut.

"Yeah, I've always drunk lots of water, but since I've been here, I haven't wanted any. So I guess we'll see if that's changed."

"Yes, we will. I'll show you where the water for drinking is." Dylan pushed the red mess of hair out of his eyes and rolled his shoulders. He was like a tiny adult with the openness of a child. "Do you want to go inside now? I think I've told you enough so you won't seem slow or dumb to anyone who meets you," he said without a hint of humor.

Coral held back a reprimand. He'd take some getting used to. "Thank you for telling me as much as you did, Dylan. I have a lot to think over and absorb. I'd love to see our house." He was going to be a handful, as Aunt Ruby would say.

"Gladly, and Coral, I'm glad you're here."

Coral pulled him into a hug. "I'm happy to be here and have a brother."

Dylan seemed uncomfortable and stiff, like any other little boy forced into a hug by his big sister. Good, maybe he wasn't all that different besides having a dragon, a flying cat, and a lack of humor tinged with bluntness. Perhaps it had to do with being the grandson of the leader too. She shrugged and squeezed the excess water out of her hair. Then she nervously brushed off her bathing suit and wiped her feet at the front door as Dylan pushed his way around her.

Chapter 26
Home Sweet Home

S he studied the swing that hung from a gold frame on the wraparound porch. *It must be a big job here to be a metalworker with all the gold.* The swing had light blue, soft-looking pads in a golden shell frame— the perfect place to read.

Dylan tapped her arm. "You should watch this."

"Watching."

Dylan held his hand up to the door. A soft yellow light scanned it, and then a deep voice spoke. "Welcome, Dylan, please enter and be happy."

"Hold your hand up as I did."

Coral did what her brother had shown her. The yellow light scanned her hand. "Guest of Dylan, please state who you are."

"I'm Coral, his sister."

"Please confirm, Dylan."

"She is my sister."

"Confirmed and stored. Welcome, Coral, and be happy."

"I will, thank you."

Dylan frowned at her. "Why are you thanking the door? It's only our security. It's not real, you know."

"I was being polite."

He nodded. "Polite. That's something I'm supposed to work on. I'll try to remind you what to do so you're polite and let you know when you don't have to be."

"Thank you, Dylan." Coral bit her lip so she wouldn't burst out laughing. What would the Pennys make of him?

173

"Follow me, and I'll take you to your room."

Coral nodded. As they crossed over the heavy gold threshold, the first room she saw took her breath away. Although the layout was similar to her old house and included a fireplace, there were many fancy upgrades too. Her eyes were drawn to all her mom's sketches, including one of her when she was eight. It was of the day her parents left on the plane, and she was clutching her necklace. There were more drawings of a baby and then the three of them in a boat.

The L-shaped blue couch was loaded with pillows and faced the fireplace, which appeared unused. There was no holder for wood or fireplace accessories, nor was there any wood stacked nearby like they used to have at their house in Nevada. But it did look like the perfect place for the family to gather.

"Do you have movies here?"

"Movies? Yes, of course. We have lots of entertainment. See that outline on the wall? That's our screen. Our whole world is connected. Mom and Dad like to have a family night when we gather here and watch stories together."

"I remember movie nights with Mom and Dad. I'll be glad to do them again. You have popcorn?"

"We do not have corn here to pop, but Mom makes a great snack you'll like."

"Guess I have a few things to get used to."

Dylan raised his eyebrows. "You do."

Coral held back a giggle. "What about the fireplace? Do you burn fires? You said it gets cool here."

"Fires again? No fires, but we use brine heat that is purple or blue, depending. And yes, it can get cold, as I said." Dylan moved through the room like a tiny soldier. "Don't worry. I'll show you all of this, Coral."

"Thanks." She ran her hand across one of the smooth gold end tables. She loved the mermaid lamps perched on top. The floor reminded her of tile, except she was walking on clear squares filled with what looked like semiprecious stones in a gold base. All this wealth was why people wanted to find this place so badly. They would dismantle all this beauty and sell it to the highest bidder. The walls sparkled with reflections from the gold, and blue drapes framed each window.

Coral couldn't help herself—she touched everything. "Are mermaids real? I mean we aren't merfolks are we?"

"Mermaids and merfolks? Oh, that's right, air people think they're real. They aren't, you know. Humans are humans, and fish are fish, not half-and-half combined. It wouldn't work."

"Oh, well, I wasn't sure. I mean, I didn't know there was a golden city underwater either." Coral grinned.

"We aren't underwater. Only our entrance to Earth is. As for the merfolks, it makes Grandma mad that people believe in them. She thinks air people aren't very sane. They believe in all kinds of crazy stuff that isn't real." Dylan stood tall and firm like her grandmother.

Coral couldn't hold back any longer and burst out laughing. He stood with his arms folded, which only made her laugh harder. Finally she got control of herself again.

"Sorry, this is all a lot to take in, Dylan."

"I know it is. That's why I waited."

She took a deep breath and ran her fingers through her tangled hair, calming herself. She already loved her know-it-all little brother. "Thank you for being patient with me. You know, Grandma doesn't seem, well, very easy to get to know."

"It's because she's a ruler. Don't worry, she ended up liking Dad, and you're her granddaughter."

She smiled. "Okay, I won't worry. Thanks, little bro."

"Little what?" He looked very puzzled, scrunching his face together.

"'Bro' is short for brother. Something us crazy air people say." Coral crossed her eyes at him.

"Well, you aren't an air person. Thank you for the new information. Are your eyes bothering you?"

"No, silly. It's something we do as a joke. You have jokes here, right?"

"Yes, we do. I can do that too, you know." Dylan crossed his eyes and even smiled. Then he abruptly turned and headed down a hall. "Come on, I'll show you more."

"Lead the way." They started down a pastel hall lined with shells embedded in the golden walls, creating a dazzling effect. She ran her hand along the walls and was surprised to find them smooth and even.

Dylan guided Coral to a green room and pointed. "This is yours. It has everything you need, including a shower and stuff."

"Really? It's beautiful."

It was filled with books—several with her mom's name on them that Coral didn't recognize. The room had a small, clear square in the wall over a gold desk. A framed drawing of Coral from when she was eight sat on the desk. Next to that was a drawing of the rest of her family. Coral's name was etched into the wall with flowers surrounding it. A dolphin and a turtle were drawn above her bed and on its headboard. Coral smiled. It was perfect. She took the waterproof bag off her shoulder and removed her camera, cell phone, gifts, and her mom's book. Thankfully, they'd survived the journey. She carefully added her things to her desk and left the rest to give to the Pennys later.

"Aren't you coming in, Dylan?"

"It's *polite* to wait to be asked."

"I'm asking you."

"Thanks. You can do whatever you want in your room. Mom and Dad won't care. They let me paint my ceiling black and add the stars to make an accurate winter night."

"That sounds cool."

"It is. Is this one of Mom's old books?" Dylan picked it up.

"Yes, it was the last book she had published before she left. I thought she might like to see it." Coral grinned. Now she would find out if her brother knew how to play.

She ran across the room and jumped on her fluffy green bed. It was soft and smelled exactly like roses on a hot summer day, and the mattress was soft and enveloped her.

This is what floating on clouds would feel like.

She waited to see what Dylan would do as she bounced around.

"Coming in. Look out!" Dylan called as he ran and jumped on the bed next to her. She giggled and tickled him, which made him hyper. Yes, there was the typical little boy, no matter how smart he was. Coral felt like everything in her life was perfect right now, and she couldn't wait for her parents to get home. She continued wrestling with her little brother, who was giggling as much as she was.

***

Ruby watched her mother as Dylan and Coral walked away. Her pride in them was evident, but she had no idea how her own reunion with her mother would go.

"I want you to meet our leader, Sabella," Emerald presented the Pennys, who had removed their scuba gear.

"Pleased to meet you." Mrs. Penny curtsied and thrust her hand out to shake.

Sabella smiled and took the offered hand. "We don't curtsey, but a slight head bow is customary. It's nice to meet you."

"Yes, we're glad to be here." Mr. Penny bowed his head and held out a hand. Sabella shook it.

Sabella smiled at the Pennys. "We're glad you were able to visit us."

Ben and Beth offered their hands, and she took them both at once. "Welcome, children."

"Thank you," they replied together, adding a nod.

Ruby watched and waited. She wanted to rush into her mother's arms, but she remembered how they'd fought when she left. It was like being that eighteen-year-old girl again waiting for her mother to acknowledge her. Ruby had been headstrong and more outspoken than her sister. She'd said some cruel things she wasn't sure her mother had forgiven.

Sabella's final words to her were still so clear in her mind. "Nothing good will come of this, Ruby. You will see it. I remove myself from any blame for what is to come. You do this against my wishes, and you won't be finishing your education as your sister did. If you go, you'll lose your place in my heart."

Unfortunately, her mother had been right about things not going well, except for her sister meeting her husband and having Coral. The worst part of her homecoming was that Jade and her father—the two people who had backed her decision to go—weren't standing next to her mother. The family had paid a steep price for their excursion into the air world.

"Ruby." Her mother finally spoke directly to her, startling her from her musings. "Please forgive the foolishness of our last words to each other. I've done nothing but regret what I said to you. I've never stopped loving or missing you. I've waited with a heavy heart until I could get you and my granddaughter back. This will be a day of celebration for years to come. Tonight I will sleep fully for the first time since you left here." Sabella held out her arms.

"Mom, I've missed you." Tears ran down Ruby's face as she ran into her mother's arms.

"Not as much as I missed you," Sabella replied. "Let's go back to the palace. Your old clothes and room are waiting for you. We have much to talk about. Penny family, you can clean up there too. We'll discuss your future after our meal tonight. I understand you need to be healed?" She directed this to Mrs. Penny.

"Yes, I do."

"We can discuss this after dinner too. Let's get back and start planning for the celebration."

Ruby wiped away her tears and suddenly wondered what would happen to the Pennys. She hoped her mother had changed, but she knew she would learn nothing more until after dinner. It was their custom.

"Come, Ruby and Emerald. Let's walk together so our city can see we are reunited."

Ruby cringed. Was her mother pointedly ignoring her sister's husband or just trying to show off her daughters? She turned and smiled at the Pennys encouragingly. Morgan winked at her. He didn't look offended. Perhaps it would be okay. Her father had been the kind and patient one, while her mother ruled. The pain of knowing she wasn't going to see him or her brother again was still so deep. She had a lot to think about and process as she walked along the golden path.

Ben took his sister's hand. She knew how he felt about her niece, but she wasn't so sure her mother would approve of that. Ruby had a feeling Coral was going to be more of a challenge than either she or Emerald had been. It would be interesting. Her excitement grew with every step closer to the castle. She couldn't wait to get back and hoped old friends would be waiting for her. She blushed as they headed toward a familiar building—*home*.

Chapter 27
A Flower in Name Only

Ned carefully approached the boat. His caution was what made him such a good soldier and employee. He couldn't wait to put faces to the voices he'd spoken to for so many years. He spotted a female on the deck who had to be Lilly Dunning. She was as lovely as he'd imagined her to be from the sultry voice. A man was coming up behind her. Ned tensed. It was Aaron, Ruby's boyfriend! That was the other Dunning? He was ready to act if anything seemed out of place. Aaron patted Lilly's back, and she smiled. He went back into working mode, tied the boat to the stairs, and climbed aboard, ready to finish his job.

There was no greeting, although Lilly's eyes said hello. He was positive she'd fallen in love with him during their phone conversations, just like he had with her. She couldn't tell him yet, but there were strong hints that a declaration of her affection was coming soon. He was good at reading people, and she was an open book to him. Luckily, a beautiful and rich open book. Lilly whispered into her brother's ear, and Aaron frowned. Did they know he'd lost Coral, Ruby, Emerald, and the Penny family? No, how could they? Then Lilly smiled at him.

"That took you forever, Ned. You know who we are, correct?" she asked in that enchanting voice.

"Yes."

Aaron grinned. "To think you wanted to kill one of your bosses. Funny now, isn't it?"

"Uh, no, well, I didn't know, sir."

"No, you didn't, Ned." Lilly's smile soothed him. "This is the end of the assignment now." She looked at her brother and raised her eyebrows.

He understood and pulled out his gun and aimed at the target's heart. Another gun went off right as he pulled the trigger. Ned was confident his shot had been a direct hit as he collapsed to the ground in a fog of slow motion. Aaron was on the ground, unmoving.

I'm shot. Why didn't Lilly stop him? I know she loves me, and I love her. Now she'll miss me.

He had so many questions, but nothing came out of his mouth. He blinked over and over, watching Lilly hold her brother's head. "I'm sorry, Aaron, but we both can't run this company." She glanced over to Ned and put her finger across her lips. "Thank you, Ned. I need your silence right now. Then I'll help you."

He nodded at her and watched her set Aaron's gun on the table. She burst into tears when a ruddy, bald man ran to her side holding a wrench.

***

"What happened, Ms. Dunning?" the captain asked as he bent over Aaron. He checked his pulse and grimly told her, "I'm sorry. He's dead." He moved over to Ned. "This one's still alive. I'll call the helicopter and get him to the hospital."

"No hurry. He killed my brother." Lilly had composed a perfect picture of heartbreak, down to the quivering lip.

"I have to report this," the captain quietly informed her.

"Yes, of course." Lilly shed more tears and held the captain's gaze at the same time.

"What should I tell the authorities?" He frowned slightly as he looked around the boat and gnawed a fingernail.

"The truth. This man came on board. When we asked him what he wanted, he pulled out a gun and shot Aaron. Luckily Aaron was cleaning his own gun, or I'd be dead too. He saved my life. Make sure they know that. It's important because he's a hero." Lilly sank down next to her brother. "Please leave me alone to say goodbye. You understand, right?"

"Yes, I understand." The captain kicked Ned's gun away from him.

Ned groaned but didn't try to speak. He trusted her.

"Good thinking. Now I need to get back to my brother, thank you."

"Call me if you need anything, and I'm very sorry for your loss." The captain threw a look at Ned one more time before shaking his head and rushing off.

Lilly had no intention of leaving a witness, and time was limited. She pulled on gloves, giving the captain enough time to call in the shooting as she picked up Ned's gun. A quick wink to Ned while putting her index finger across her lips, then came the scream. On cue the captain arrived at a run.

He was breathing hard and clutching his chest by the time he got to her. "Are you okay?"

"Why, yes, I am." Lilly smiled, holding the gun behind her.

The captain eyed her warily and stepped back. "I called in the shooting, Ms. Dunning."

"Oh, good. Thank you. I appreciate all you've done for me." She stood directly over Ned.

"I'm just doing my job. I should get back to the radio. Call if you need anything," The captain backed away slowly, his body tense.

Lilly changed her posture, slouching and widening her eyes in a defeated stance. "Wait. Can you take this with you?"

"Yes, Ms. Dunning, what—"

She raised the gun and shot the captain twice before he could finish. His eyes bulged out like overfilled balloons as he crumpled to the deck. She took Ned's hand, emptied the gun in the captain's direction, and then checked him. No heartbeat. She placed the gun next to Ned and stroked his cheek, smiling.

***

Ned smiled back at Lilly. His pain was gone. He felt a small glimmer of hope. He heard a weak version of his voice. "Finally we're together. I love you and can't wait—"

Lilly held her hand up. "Well, I'm flattered, of course, but you see, I was lucky to escape a crazy stalker who killed my brother. It only got worse for me when I had to use my brother's gun to shoot this stalker after he killed the boat's captain. My bad—I didn't move your gun away from you, but it's to be expected after such a shock. You must understand I can't be a suspect, right? You have been an asset to our team. Thank you, Ned, from the bottom of my heart." She aimed and fired.

"Wait—" Ned's voice sounded so far away. He heard the shot but felt nothing. Now she'd never know what happened with Coral, Ruby, Emerald, and the Pennys.

Good.

Then everything faded away.

***

Lilly watched him take his last breath, threw her brother's gun down, and tucked the gloves into her pocket to throw away the first chance she got. Time for an award-winning performance. It would certainly help that she knew the right people to speed this investigation along in her favor. She sat next to her brother and waited for help or one of the divers to arrive. It seemed like it took forever, but finally they surfaced. She sprang into action.

The first diver out of the water pulled off his mask as his mouth fell open. "What happened?" He quickly tossed his gear aside and rushed to her.

"It was horrible—my brother!" She sobbed and threw herself on Aaron.

The second diver didn't stop to remove anything, hurrying to her side. "You weren't shot or injured?"

"No, my brother was," Lilly informed them quietly.

"I don't feel a pulse," the first diver informed her through a tight frown.

"I know, he's dead!" Lilly cried, holding her head. There, that had to look like she was completely grief-stricken.

"The other two?" the second diver gently asked, leaning over her. Water dripped on her like tears.

"The captain and the shooter—I'm not sure if they're alive." She put her hand to her throat.

The second diver didn't leave her side while the first checked for life. She stole a glance as he put his muscular arm around her. He was good looking in a surfer type of way. He'd make a nice distraction later. He covered her with a towel from the lounge and scanned the waters. He was buying it.

"All three are dead," the other diver, who was more on the well-fed side, informed them with a grim expression. "I'm going to secure the boat and call this in. You stay here with her."

Lilly continued sobbing while the man gently held her. She enjoyed their moment together before the first one came back.

"All clear, and help is coming. Can you tell us what happened, Ms. Dunning?"

"It doesn't seem real to me . . . " She glanced at the handsome diver, who smiled encouragingly at her. He had the most beautiful brown eyes she could get lost in. All of these divers had military training and were single. Her brother had insisted on that. For once he'd done something right, because this was going to be her next personal bodyguard. She started her practiced scenario of a stalker coming to kill her but instead killing everyone else. She finished with a loud sob. "It was like a nightmare coming to life."

"I know this is a horrible shock for you, Ms. Dunning," the first diver said. "Can I get you something?"

She shook her head and wiped away the tears.

"You're safe now." The second diver smiled and added, "And help should be here any moment."

Lilly held back a smile. "Thank you, both of you. I don't even know your names."

"Stuart Mann, ma'am," number one said.

"Rob Quail."

"Thank you, Stuart and Rob. I don't know what I'd have done if you hadn't shown up when you did," Lilly added with a sigh.

"No problem," Rob replied. Stuart said something too, but honestly, she wasn't listening to him.

She took a deep breath and ran her fingers through her hair. "This is hard for me to deal with, but it has to be done. I know my brother had confidentiality contracts with his employees because of our dealings with the government. He lost his life bravely, like any soldier, and I need you to honor your promise and the mission. As far as anyone knows, we are studying whales to improve our products. As for Ms. Hyde, traitor to our great country, that information is not to be divulged. The story will be that Aaron's girlfriend tumbled off the boat when the shooting started. We couldn't save or find her. The rest of the narrative follows the truth and will honor a great hero—Aaron."

Stuart stood tall and saluted Aaron. "I understand, ma'am. I'll proudly honor Mr. Dunning."

"Understood." Rob nodded. He stayed and comforted her while Stuart handled the radio.

Yes. They believed every word.

Later, so did the authorities.

Lilly made her plans while being escorted off the boat. There would be a sabbatical to recover. She'd already signed Rob on to come with her—to keep her safe. Then she'd start the search again, going over every inch of this area. She wouldn't stop until she found the golden city. If she had to start dropping bombs to get their attention, she would. At least there was still the Penny family. There wasn't any doubt that they knew more than they let on. Money wasn't a problem now with her backstabbing, penny-pinching brother out of the way. At only thirty-five years old, time was on her side, and she would get what she wanted.

Chapter 28
Dinner at the Castle

Coral, Dylan, and her parents were escorted into a massive dining room. Coral felt almost like a beautiful princess. For the first time, she was glad to have Beth to share this with. She nervously smoothed the soft blue material of her amazing dress. It exposed her arms and belly but covered her legs to the ankle. It was soft and flowy, which was how she would describe the room.

The golden walls were etched with murals. Long lines reminded her of flower stems bending in an unseen current. Fish and a coral reef completed the first wall. The second wall had a dolphin pod swimming through a kelp bed with a humpback whale in the background. She wondered how long it had taken to carve these images into the gold walls and then add amazing color to them. An octopus with a group of turtles feeding underneath it in a kelp forest took up another wall. The octopus took a protective stance over the turtles, unlike the one who'd held her parents captive.

The fourth wall had people in three frames, much like newspaper comics. In the first panel were people wearing clothes similar to her family's. They were watching smoke off in the distance. The next one was a group of people riding on the back of dolphins, just like she had, except they held up long sticks like weapons. They appeared to be going into the cave that led here. The final picture showed people walking out of the water onto a sandy beach in tattered clothes. Some looked injured.

The Great War?

Huge, sparkling chandeliers that looked like they were made from diamonds filled the room with a soft glow. The light, from actual candles, reflected off the pearls and shells on the gold table, making it the best part of the incredible room. The table was long, with carved legs that reminded her of Roman pillars. Everything shone and glowed, including the shell-shaped dishes with a finish like the inside of an abalone shell—except more colorful. Flowers she had never seen before graced the table like a circular neon rainbow.

There were massive amounts of food piled in the middle of the table on three enormous platters. Coral hoped it tasted better than it looked. The first platter was filled with a bright orange paste. The green chunks on platter two were even less appealing. The third one had a creamy white sauce over what looked like fish. It may have looked weird, but at least it smelled good, like eating flowers for dinner. She tried to remain hopeful.

A beautiful, dark-haired young woman in red led her to a chair across from her mom and the rest of the family. "Wait for Her Majesty to sit first." She didn't make eye contact.

"Thank you."

No response.

"She isn't trained to respond to the family, only listen and instruct if needed. It is the custom for your grandmother to enter a silent room," Emerald whispered.

Coral decided she'd want the people working for her to talk. The Penny family caught her attention as they entered and were led to their chairs. Three of the Pennys were next to her, and Ben was placed next to her brother. They were solemnly instructed to stand and wait in silence. Finally, Aunt Ruby came in and stood on Coral's other side.

They all had the same style of clothing. The women's dresses reminded Coral of the costume she wore for her mermaid dance, all in soft pastels. The men had on long, flowy pants in darker colors like navy, red, and black, but no shirts. Both Mr. Penny and Ben looked uncomfortable as they hunched forward, but her dad seemed to embrace this style, standing tall. Of course, he'd had more time to get used to it.

Tara would have loved this. A heavy wave of sadness passed over Coral. How was Tara reacting to her drowning and the Pennys and her aunt disappearing? Would it be declared an accident at sea while they were looking for her? That made the most sense, but she hoped Tara would know, on some level, that Coral's dream had come true.

Shifting from foot to foot in her snug golden sandals, she watched Ben take in the grand room. She grinned when their eyes connected. He wiggled his eyebrows at her and glanced down at her dress. He seemed to enjoy what she was wearing just as much as she liked his shirtless outfit. She blushed and looked away. She attempted to run her fingers through her hair, but they met with the French braid her mom had insisted on. It was the first time Coral and Beth had the same hairstyle.

She focused on Dylan fussing with his dark blue pants like a caterpillar trying to get out of its cocoon. Dressing up was never comfortable, and she didn't want to float around in this type of dress daily, no matter who her grandma was or how pretty it made her feel.

She stole another look at Ben. It was his turn to redden. Dylan cleared his throat and rolled his eyes toward the end of the table. It was time.

"Her Royal Majesty, Queen Sabella," announced the same doe-eyed girl that had helped Coral to her seat.

Sabella seated herself and said, "Please sit down."

The chairs were gold and had high backs with scalloped edges like seashells. They had soft blue, padded backs and seats, and the feet matched the table. Coral expected the chair to be comfortable, but it was hard, like sitting on a park bench, with no give at all. It didn't move easily, so she had to slip into it as she had seen her grandmother do. She hoped this wasn't going to be a long dinner. Her mom nodded to the napkin on the plate, which was folded to look like a fan. Coral quickly opened it and placed it over her lap.

Sabella offered a small smile and picked up her fluted cup. "Thank you for joining me for my meal. It is a great honor for me. We'll raise our glasses to honor our guests and for the safe return of my daughter and granddaughter." She nodded to the people in red, who quickly poured a purple liquid into their cups. She held her cup high and laid her other hand on her heart. "May our hearts shine bright, our health be strong, and our intentions as pure as our gold."

"All of us," Coral's parents and aunt responded and drank.

Coral glanced at Ben as she sniffed the sour liquid he was already drinking. Dylan was the only one who'd gotten something else. It reminded her of the wine they'd tried at Tara's house a couple of weeks ago—she hadn't liked it. Coral's mom nudged her, so she took a sip. It was cool like water but sour like candy. It was nothing like red wine. Beth leaned back and caught Coral's eye as she wrinkled her nose. Coral mouthed *Try it.*

Beth shook her head, and Coral lost sight of her behind her parents again, but she could see the glass was back on the table. She drank hers in three gulps. A person promptly came to refill their cups.

Emerald held up her hand. "That is all these kids will have, thank you." She whispered to Coral, "It's our traditional celebration drink, like champagne. Until you're an adult, in three years, you'll only get one glass on special occasions. And this is very special, trust me." She smiled.

Her mom looked beautiful in a green dress that matched her eyes. A smaller version of the crown set on her grandmother's thick gray hair was perched on her head. It had pearls, rubies, and emeralds, just like on their floor at home. Coral had been given a diamond-and-sapphire barrette shaped like tree branches to wear in her hair. It was heavy on her head and a sign of who she was. It was a responsibility that she wasn't sure she wanted.

"I kind of liked it." Coral smiled. She didn't feel any different. Dylan was getting a refill of a clear liquid, and she got the same thing. It was sparkly and tasted a lot like apple juice with a kick.

"It's not something you want to drink a lot of at once. You won't feel good later. Trust me." Her mom added a wink.

Morgan interrupted. "I'm so glad you're home. You have no idea how much we missed you."

"I have a very good idea." Coral giggled.

Hey, maybe she was feeling that drink after all. It was the first time in eight years she'd felt this happy, so why worry about it?

Sabella's loud voice interrupted any conversations with a command. "Serve the food now."

The people in red picked up the platters and quickly began serving. Each plate got some white, green, and orange goop, carefully arranged so they didn't touch. Coral's parents, Dylan, and her aunt dove right into the food. Her dad was smacking his lips. She was okay trying the white stuff, but that pasty orange? What was it?

Dylan caught her eye and held his fork up to his mouth. She mimicked her little brother and first ate what she thought was fish. The white stuff wasn't fish. It was like nothing she had ever tasted before. It did melt in her mouth, although it wasn't warm, as she'd expected—it was room temperature. Its texture and taste were more like mashed potatoes slathered in butter and gravy, just like at Thanksgiving.

"This is good!" she exclaimed.

Dylan shook his head at her and put a finger to his lips.

"Sorry," she mumbled.

She glanced over to Ben, who smiled at her and took a taste of the green stuff. He made a quick face when no one was looking, and she had to suppress a giggle. She spooned some into her mouth. It was amazing, like her mom's split pea soup, but cold.

All she and Ben had left was the orange stuff.

Coral scooped some onto her fork. She raised her eyebrows at Ben and waited for him to do the same thing. Her lips shaped a countdown—one, two, three—and she put it in her mouth, expecting it to taste like that poi at the luau. It didn't. Instead, it was like all her favorite fruits blended, like a tropical smoothie. Ben gave her a quick wink and cleaned his plate. Seconds were offered, which she declined. The meal was surprisingly filling.

Her first meal with her royal family was a success. Dylan made a clicking sound to capture her attention. He nodded toward their grandmother as the plates were quietly taken away. Her face was pinched like Aunt Ruby's used to be when she reprimanded her. She lifted a hand as all faces turned to her.

"I hope you all enjoyed your meal."

"Yes, thank you. It was wonderful." Mrs. Penny spoke up.

"Yes—" Coral started, but Dylan shook his head at her and mouthed *Don't talk now.*

Sabella held her hand up, and again the room went silent. "I'm glad you enjoyed it, and we'll enjoy our after-meal treat in a moment. First, I want you to know I watched what went on above on that boat after Coral and Ruby left it." She paused and looked at Coral. "We can do that besides dream-watch, Coral, if we aren't sealed in and the people are on the ocean or any body of water. The water birds become our eyes and ears. Water conducts our energy is a simple explanation. You'll learn much more about that soon." She continued with the same pinched expression as she quickly updated them on what had happened on the boat.

Coral gasped, only to have Dylan warn her by putting a hand over his mouth.

Sabella sighed and finished. "So, it seems Ms. Dunning got away with what she did. Although two of the three people who meant us harm are dead, we still must worry about this Lilly Dunning. She's willing to do anything to find us, so soon we'll have to close our door to Earth. Which some of you know will prevent us from seeing what goes on there. I did not want to give you such unpleasant news before you had a chance to eat. It is not our way to disturb our eating with talk." Sabella looked directly at Coral again. "You have many new things to learn, Coral. I know your parents and brother will teach you what is expected of you. You'll learn we must always be prepared to make tough decisions when the time arises." She paused with a deep frown, then sat a little straighter and avoided looking at the Penny family.

Uh-oh.

"This is one of those times. I'm not comfortable having more air people living with us. I understand that Sarah Penny needs our assistance, and of course, we'll provide it. The rest of the family, however, should go back to their kind. We'll make them forget before they go, don't worry. Then—"

"Wait," Coral interrupted. "You mean you're going to keep Mrs. Penny here and send her family away?"

"Coral," her mom urgently whispered, shaking her head. "Don't interrupt her, please."

"It's all right, Emerald—this time. She needs to know things, and I'm willing to tell her. Yes, I'm not so cruel as to let her die, and she will if she leaves. She's done no wrong, nor has her daughter. I could let the daughter stay, but her husband and son are not pure of heart, like them. I do not wish them to stay."

"You didn't wish my husband to stay with me either, if you'll remember," Emerald said quietly.

"Well, there was one time I agreed to change my mind, and it provided me with beautiful grandchildren."

"If I may speak." Mrs. Penny raised her hand.

Sabella nodded. "Please do."

Mrs. Penny looked at her husband, who was shaking his head at her. Then she smiled at her kids. "I said this before, that I'd rather die soon and spend my last few moments with my husband and children than stay here without them. I will not change my mind on this."

Sabella studied her closely. "If that is what you want, then we will take you back up top in the morning. I will retire for the evening. Stay here and enjoy the after-dinner treats, please. I'll see you all here in the morning at breakfast. Thank you for joining me. Rest well."

190

"Grandmother, wait!" Coral blurted out. "You must reconsider this. They're decent people. I understand why they did this. They didn't hurt me. Mr. Penny saved Aunt Ruby's life, and Ben saved mine. I don't see why they can't stay here. They're good people who made some bad decisions. Everyone makes mistakes. I'm sure you have too, right?" She immediately wished she could take those last few words back.

Her mom and Aunt Ruby gasped. "That is enough, Coral," her mom said. "No one talks to your grandmother like that, *ever*. I'm sorry, Mother. She doesn't understand."

Sabella turned around and stared at her. Coral mumbled, "I'm sorry, Grandmother," but in a clear, firm voice, she added, "but I don't want to see them go. They're my friends, and I can forgive them. They took care of me when my parents weren't there. They were family to Aunt Ruby and me. Right, Aunt Ruby?"

Aunt Ruby nodded weakly. Why was everyone so afraid of her grandmother? What would she do to them—or her? Coral glanced around the table. Mrs. Penny leaned forward and mouthed *Thank you*. Beth had tears in her eyes. Ben and Mr. Penny were staring at her grandmother. Dylan was the only one who offered her an encouraging smile.

Sabella's face was neutral, but the fire came through her eyes. "Do you believe I'm wrong now, Coral?"

D. L. Finn

Chapter 29
Challenging a Queen

C oral's mouth suddenly felt like a desert as she planted her feet and set her shoulders, "Um . . . no. I was just telling you how I felt. My mom and I invited them to stay with us. Wouldn't we be going back on our word now? I mean, shouldn't we honor our promises?"

"Well, Coral, I will admit to having been wrong once or twice. You may have crossed our lines of etiquette, but you have made a valid point. Since the promise to the Pennys was made by your mother, who is the leader-in-training, and by you, the heir, and her word carries almost as much power as mine, I must agree with you. What I have just witnessed makes me feel confident that you will speak up when you see wrongdoing. I'm pleased." Sabella smiled brightly, and the room breathed out like a gust of wind blowing away the tension.

She turned her attention to the Pennys. "The original offer stands. If you choose to live with us, know that you can't leave here. Although, honestly, I doubt you'll want to. Our world is just as big as the air world. We don't hurt anyone, nor do we quest for money or power like you are used to. We work together, and you'll have a lot to learn. Your children will be raised as our own. And, most important, you will be friends of our house. Can you honor that and our way of life here?"

Mr. Penny stood up. "Yes. We can. I thank you for this second chance for our family." He winked at Coral. "We're leaving all we had behind, but my wife is worth anything we could have had back home. I'll do whatever is required of me in this world to earn your trust and forgiveness. I promise my loyalty to this world and its people. You're giving us a great gift, and for that, I'm eternally grateful."

"Family is the greatest gift." Sabella was so quiet Coral had to strain to hear her. The queen paused for a moment, held her head up a bit higher, and brushed aside a stray hair that had escaped from her bun. She locked eyes with Mr. Penny before she continued in her normal tone. "I still grieve the loss of my husband and son, but having Coral and Ruby back has brought me peace. Sarah has shown me her strength and nobility by choosing to end her life with her family over living without them. Ben and Beth will thrive here, I'm sure. Robert, you must prove yourself to us. I know you expected that." She smiled. "Coral, if you don't mind, we can heal Sarah now, as a team. I don't want her to have another night of pain."

Coral nodded and went to stand with her grandmother.

Mrs. Penny stood up, glancing over at her husband. "Now? Will it hurt?"

"Oh, no. You'll feel it, though, and then you won't. Please sit back down. This might make you dizzy. Coral, you remember what I said about working from your core? I know you tried once before in that hotel. Please do that again. I'll add to it, and that will be enough this time. Living here will keep her healthy until it is her time, which will be a longer span than is usual in the air world. Ready?"

"Yes." Mrs. Penny blew a kiss to her family.

"Yes," Coral added.

Mr. Penny hurried to his wife's side and gently kissed her cheek before moving out of the way. Beth and Ben stood up and went to their father. Beth grasped her brother's and father's hands. They looked like they were watching a horror movie, but Coral felt calm. Her parents were smiling, and her dad and Dylan gave her a thumbs-up, looking like twins.

Aunt Ruby nodded. "You can do this."

Coral had a feeling that her grandmother changing her mind was as rare as an oasis in a desert. She looked at her for guidance. Sabella grabbed Coral's hand, and she immediately felt a surge coming out of her fingers when they touched. Together they put their hands on top of Mrs. Penny's head. Energy flowed through her body into her hands and entered Mrs. Penny. It wasn't draining—she felt stronger by the moment.

Then, like a water faucet being shut off, the energy stopped. Her grandmother removed her hands and gave Coral a slight nod. Rubbing her hands together, she stood back to see if it worked. The room was so silent she was positive she could hear Mrs. Penny's heart racing.

194

"Oh," Mrs. Penny finally said. She looked up at Coral with no expression on her face, then her eyes closed, and her head flopped down like a rag doll. Sabella deftly caught it before it hit the table and gently laid it down.

"What's wrong?" Mr. Penny lunged toward the table.

Sabella held her hand up. "Nothing. Your wife is fine now. She'll wake up in a moment a new woman, but still the woman she was. Her pure heart impressed me."

"She's healed?" Mr. Penny's upper body was flushed.

"Yes. Take a few deep breaths, Robert, before you pass out too."

He took those suggested breaths and then moved to his wife's side. "Thank you. I am not sure I will ever be able to repay you or Coral for this."

"It was our pleasure, right, Coral?"

"Yes, it was. Thank you, Grandmother."

Mrs. Penny's eyes fluttered open and immediately found her husband's anxious stare. She smiled. Mr. Penny's face lit up with a happiness that would rival the brightest of lights. "Thank you." He drew her into his arms with a contented sigh.

"Sarah will now have so much energy. I believe her skills could be put to good use as our family's personal shopper. We have so little time to acquire the things we need. Don't you think, Ruby?" Sabella asked.

"That might just work, Mother." Ruby smiled.

Just then a wide-eyed man rushed into the room and immediately caught Ruby's attention.

"Bard?" She gasped.

He clasped his hand to his heart. "It's true! You're really here!"

"I am."

"I was out of town but got here the minute I heard. I've waited seventeen long years for you to come back to me." His voice quavered, and his eyes were full of tears. He was tall and radiated kindness in a way that made him very attractive. He brushed back his bright red hair and looked at her aunt like Mr. Penny looked at Mrs. Penny. Aunt Ruby had had someone who loved her this whole time.

"I can't believe you waited all these years. I know we agreed to get engaged when I got back, but of course, I don't hold you to that."

"Well, I hold you to it, Ruby. I still want you as my wife, if you'll have me." He stood in front of her.

"Have you? I don't deserve you. I should never have left you in the first place, but I was young—that's my only defense."

"None of that matters now. I understood that you needed to do what you did. I didn't like it, but I understood. I've never stopped loving you, Ruby." He got down on his knees. "Will you be my wife?"

Ruby's face matched his hair as tears filled her eyes. "Yes, Bard, I'd be honored."

"Of course, with your blessings, Sabella." He bowed his head to her.

Sabella held her hands up. "You have it. I look forward to more grandchildren."

"Kids?" Ruby asked with a shyness Coral had never seen from her.

"Of course, if that's what you want."

She nodded with a huge grin on her face. Bard scooped her up in his arms and kissed her.

Everyone found themselves busy as this went on. Coral caught Ben watching her. She wondered if someday—if her grandmother would allow it. Sabella cleared her throat. The newly engaged couple pulled apart, beaming.

"Welcome to the family." Emerald hugged Bard.

"Thank you, Emerald. Is this Coral?"

"It is," Morgan replied.

"I'm so glad I finally get to meet you. I look forward to getting to know you and being your uncle." Bard bowed his head to Coral.

"I'm glad to meet you too." He was nice but was being very formal—except for that kiss.

"I hope the wedding is soon. You have some catching up to do if you want as many kids as we have." Emerald winked with a sly grin. "We're expecting our third."

"What? Really? Oh, sis. Another one! I'm so excited!"

"Another brother or sister? Cool." Coral noted that Dylan didn't seem surprised or disturbed by the idea.

Morgan put his arm around Emerald. "Yup, very cool. We just found out when you guys got back."

"My heart is full to have new and returning grandchildren fill my world," Sabella added. "I think your wedding has been postponed for too long. Let's plan it for next week—if you can help us pull it together with supplies and clothes, Sarah."

"I'd be honored," she replied.

Bard nodded so hard Coral worried he would hurt his neck. "A Christmas wedding sounds good to me. Ruby?"

"It's perfect. How about we have it on the pink hill where we used to have picnics?"

"I was just going to suggest that. Sabella, do you mind if I borrow your daughter for a bit?" He bowed his head to her again.

"Yes, please go catch up. And welcome to the family, Bard."

They rushed out of the room like giddy teens. Her parents looked so happy, and Coral realized she would be there to hold the baby this time. She smiled and hugged her parents, with Dylan squished in the middle. Sabella joined them. Her dad nodded over to the Pennys. Mrs. Penny looked ten years younger as Beth and Ben gathered around her in a huge family hug.

"I noticed how that boy looks at you," Sabella whispered to Coral. "He must prove himself to me before I could consider him as more than a friend to you. Your father has shown me I can be wrong about people, but I won't stop protecting the ones I love. You have much to learn before we speak of this again. Just know how proud I am of you, Coral, and how much I love you." She pulled Coral into a hug.

"Thank you, Grandma. I love you too. I'm thankful you're keeping an open mind about—" she saw Ben was watching them and added, "everything. I'm so happy to be here with all of you. I can't wait to learn more."

"Come, Coral. We'd better offer everyone after-dinner treats. Try the white nuggets first. They're my favorite. They compare favorably to your ice cream." Sabella took Coral's hand and reached out to Dylan with the other.

Coral smiled at her grandmother. Ben was going to be the one for her. She felt that with every part of her being, but she realized she had a lot to do before that happened. Right now, though, she had family, friends, and a new world filled with magic and wonder to explore. Even though she was determined to ruin that, Lilly wasn't going to win because they could shut their door to Earth. This place wasn't going to be perfect—nothing was— but she was ready for anything that came as long as she had her family and friends by her side. They were all that mattered to her now, and with them, she had it all.

D. L. Finn

Author's note

I hope you enjoyed Coral's journey. In addition to my love of the forest and mountains in the Sierra Nevada, where I live, Hawaii has a special place in my heart, and it has shown up more than once in my stories. This started as a short story many years ago and sat collecting dust. I must thank my family for being so patient with me as I keep meeting new characters that not only visit but move in with us for months until they go forth into the world on the pages of a book.

I'd like to thank all who helped me with this, including the staff at the airports in Reno, Honolulu, and Kahului, for all their holiday decoration information. I especially want to thank you, my readers, for taking this trip to Mearth with Coral and her family.

About the Author

D. L. Finn is an independent California local who encourages everyone to embrace their inner child. She was born and raised in the foggy Bay Area, but in 1990 she relocated with her husband, kids, dogs, and cats to Nevada City, in the Sierra foothills. She immersed herself in reading all types of books but especially loved romance, horror, and fantasy. She always treasured creating her own reality on paper. Finally, surrounded by towering pines, oaks, and cedars, her creativity was nurtured until it bloomed. Her creations include children's books, adult fiction, a unique autobiography, and poetry. She continues on her adventure with an open invitation to all readers to join her.

Made in the USA
Las Vegas, NV
30 January 2021